The Corpse Dream of N. Petkov

Thomas McGonigle

The Dalkey Archive Press, 1987

The spark for this prose came from Michael O'Riordan, head of the Communist Party of Ireland, who gave me in 1968 the book *Dimitrov Wastes No Bullets*, by Michael Padev, saying, "This is the only book in my library about Bulgaria."

Copyright © 1987 by Thomas McGonigle

ISBN: 0-916583-19-8
Library of Congress Catalog Card Number: 86-072661

First Edition

Partially funded by grants from The National Endowment for the Arts and The Illinois Arts Council

The Dalkey Archive Press
1817 79th Avenue
Elmwood Park, IL 60635 USA

The Corpse Dream of N. Petkov

Thomas McGonigle

Also by Thomas McGonigle

In Patchogue

Because of M.   *twenty-five years ago*

for R. & L.

once

on Vitosha

I learned . . .

In the election held in October the Fatherland Front won 78 percent of the votes and the opposition 22 percent. In the new government George Dimitrov became premier, with Georgiev as vice-premier and foreign minister. Elected as a representative to the assembly, Petkov openly defied the Communist leadership and attacked Dimitrov as a tool of the Soviet Union. This opposition was allowed to continue for a while because the government wished to obtain Western approval of the peace treaty, which had finally been completed. The day after the U.S. Senate ratified the agreement, in June 1947, Petkov was arrested. He was tried in August, sentenced to death, and, despite Western protests, hanged in September. One week after this event the United States officially recognized the Bulgarian government. With the completion of the destruction of the Agrarian opposition, the Communists proceeded in similar manner against those Socialist Democrats who still attempted to maintain an independent position. By the end of 1947 Bulgaria was completely under Communist control, and a new constitution was in effect.

History of the Balkans (Jelavich)

I, Nikola Petkov, was hanged by the neck and was dead, slowly, as they expected, on 23 September 1947, a poor job of it in the eyes of some, though in *their* eyes: well done, well done, the life of him squeezed out, pulled out, gasped out, one after two after three

                                 after four minutes and the life is still

five

six

seven

eight

7

nine
ten
eleven
was it
twelve minutes . . . or longer or shorter and careful not to use piano wire
because of its Hitler tune and they did not insert, contrary to legend, the
thin glass tube up my pisshole and gently tap with surgical hammer, not
that cruel, mark me   nine
                             ten minutes
with feet no longer touching the tipped-over stool, remember the white
painted stool the children sat on next to the baba—no, not painted—
unpainted, raw wood, like the beam about which my necklace is wound.

*I do not look out from my window and see gondolas rising and falling
at the dock: lumbering seaborne creatures. I do not look up and see a
man standing upon an alligator on top of a pillar. I do not hear
Swedish, Greek, German, English, French, Serb voices down there on
the sidewalk. I am not in exile in Venice. I am living on the Jewish
Rialto. Or what was once the Jewish Rialto according to the old guide-
books. In New York City. On the Island of Manhattan.*

The stool has been scuffed previously by the boots of men who step up
to open/close the high window; not to be scuffed by my feet clothed in
pieces of cloth, stinking pieces of rag—to be stood, thus, with eyes
turned down to see the yellow tops of the dirt-contoured nails but how to
be sure that is what I am seeing when I look, with these eyes, down
to . . . a flaw but hardly flaw enough to destroy though I do not reach for
poetry and its license as an excuse for these moments though here I am:
rope slick with scraped skin and dried blood . . . part of what they do so
well, wanting me to think at this moment: how ordinary they think all
this is . . . nothing so out of the ordinary, no reason enough to use a new

rope, the old one is good enough for *him* . . . who does he think he is . . . he no longer capable of thought, he only in the history books published over *there* and who will even know his name in twenty years, in 25, in 30, in 40, in 50 . . . he wasn't a sensational axe murderer stalking the newspaper of the old regime . . . rope slick with use, groaning poor rope under my weight but not enough weight to end
                                        I try to fling this story from me, but what country would have it?

Just the rope cutting into the neck's skin. I am dirtying myself. Like a child and everyone looking at me as I walk as close to the wall as possible, the shit streaming down my leg . . . no, it isn't when I look, just, I feel it coming down my leg. They can smell my shit . . . thirty years ago and right back there, still, we never get beyond the age of twelve, so someone once wrote probably under the influence of the doctor in Vienna, a man wrote, who has not read that man from Russia who
- carried a happy childhood upon his back—so people said who met him in New York . . .

Very far away. And not just measured by miles or hours. Until I go down to the street and then by subway . . . into the city, into that awful feeling: four more days of this, this week . . . I can take my pursuit of Nikola Petkov with the seriousness he deserves . . . but today hammers that seriousness . . . I have not been able to find the dimensions of his cock or whether his interests were in the opposite sex or in his own or in neither. Ah, a certain vulgarity . . .

This Might Serve as an example of dilly-dallying in the backwaters of history and coming down the pike is the semi of French-speaking confusion urging me to tighten up my interests and get on to discussing my theory of history, of historical re-creation and forget the actual man, Nikola Petkov, to forget this actual country, Bulgaria . . . which is, after all, just a word, a mere word, and it can mean anything you want it to . . .

So much is kept from us, was kept from us, even those who understood many languages . . . it was as if suddenly finding oneself dumb in both one's own language and in all the other languages of the earth
as if
as if, those were the words that can go through my head as a constant mechanical drum to whatever tune was being played by the musicians out front and in front of them the vocalist of the day . . . how easily replaceable the vocalist is . . . while acknowledging that each and every musician is replaceable . . . the only person who doesn't change is the manager . . . off there driving away with his cut before anyone else . . . the one who deals with the other managers and talks of the unruly musicians, the vocalist who has emotional problems, who can't face the audience again . . .
just give them . . . an arm is waving the imaginary looped rope.

I sat with him, through the night, the early morning and just before noon, his hand turned to ashes. That is how I wished it to be, to have been: the brother gone, the father before him in public with strangers looking on, commenting on dress and facial expression: material for the evening meal to digest along with the cabbage and potatoes joined to a technical discussion of the pistol's caliber and lack of necessity for all those bullets wasted . . . when there are enough scoundrels about to use up all the bullets ever manufactured . . . I could not entertain that idea . . . it is not in my character . . . or so they say, though I know quite well those lives lived with no other purpose than to serve those who like to see their enemies launched into the next world.

Let God settle all the final scores. We're keeping track of the here and now.

So many hands held . . . what a luxury . . . how we will look back upon those days when men and women died in bed with their hands held. Now, as if each was waiting for the puff of wind to scatter them, as if they had been no more than a speck of ash, burned newspaper, waiting to explode into the air.

Only the honing of the knives as their memorial. And sound does not linger except in the reports of young journalists in love with the singer.

Mouth fills with words that close the eyes for why in all that is . . . would anyone living in New York City in the year, say, 1983, is that not a year far enough away from the dangle of this rope . . . would anyone be interested in the fate of the leader of the Bulgarian Agrarian Union . . . just three words and I see the eye glaze over with sleep as if I had concentrated the *Goldberg Variations* into three words . . . a certain achievement . . . my tongue spasmodically moving, fanning no sounds into words, just knowing with the squeezing of liquid between tongue and roof of mouth that I had better tell you where Bulgaria is: north of Greece, east of Yugoslavia, west of Romania sort of, and sort of south of Hungary . . . east of Italy and south of France, I guess, and all just very far from where these words are being recorded . . . but not far from where they originate . . . but every Bulgarian desires to flee . . . no, only the rulers who are German, according to another American who was not sympathetic to our people . . . liking the skirts of the Greek soldiers . . . eight hours by plane to London, from here on the Jewish Rialto . . . then, what, four hours more by plane if you can get one, or three nights on the train when it runs from Victoria Station . . . . . . because we must travel by train into ancient history—as far back as figures out of, or almost Herodotus   into——thud——*our people.*

They would have us always looking *out there* for a way to live, a way to think, a way to copulate. We were to take instruction: never were we to find anything of value within our own experience. They always know better. Most of the time, it is said, it can be argued that they were right. But still, the eyes grow weak and useless if they are always used for looking to the distance. There has to be some variety. How simple this sounds. And they have said that also. Simple, naive—just a bunch of peasants.

If we could fly to Paris, walk to the Pont Nord, fill our eyes with impressionist paint.

If our hands could be emptied of the knife slitting the belly of the pig to be upended legs hauled to the sky

I can not sustain this litany of self-hatred . . . can not sustain it even for the sake of argument. Letters would come back from *there*, it does not matter where *there* is, just from there and everybody always has a there in their own history. It is always better *there*. As simple as that: it is always better *there* just because it is not here. The hand I was dealt. Done with, no ground to revise. At a certain age everything is done and you just have to act it out, the lines so familiar, so chewed over that a toothless man could . . .

In December 1944—6 weeks after his return from Moscow—the Communists informed Petkov that I would have to resign as general secretary of the party, or else. Realizing there was no alternative at this stage and in an attempt to gain time, I handed over my office to Petkov, whom the Communists made clear they favored. For his part, he still believed he could effect a reconciliation with them. So, Dr. Georgi M. Dimitrov, the anti-Soviet fanatic, had been removed, and Nikola Petkov, life-long friend of the Soviets, had taken my place. In a speech on January 21, 1945—the day of my withdrawal—Communist Vice Premier Dobre Tarpeshev gushed. "If I were a woman, I can think of no one I would rather marry than Nikola Petkov."

No flower just beyond reach, nor toss of hair or pig grunting behind weathered unpainted board fence or goose being led by ribbon for a walk along the street . . . and no field of snow, that old reliable setting beloved of all Russians or those filled with the books, waiting in Varna for crest of wave to fill the long winter with . . . would all come soon enough when they turn this place into a packaged holiday, after removing, with refined logic, the models for the imitation peasants whom they will set behind factory-made folk tables to manufacture folk items for the tourists to take back to their rooms in Dusseldorf to eventually move from right there in front of their eyes to remind them of this year's holiday and as the year goes on . . . moved further and further to why are we holding on to this junk, do you think anybody would give us something for it?

Should a splinter get into my toe, would I be able to feel it . . . I do feel it in spite of this being written years later . . . when it would seem a convention more of literature to feel a splinter and not the rope about my neck . . . though after the event that is all we have: the conventions of literature. And there we have the we—the famous *we*. They have won, if a pronoun can be used as a symbol. I will have to consult the French and Russians on this matter: I am sure it is okay to use a pronoun as a symbol though there might just be a theory that abrogates it. Got to have something material . . . like the side of Jesus as a handwarmer on a sudden chilled spring day.

Hand grabbing the waist of my trousers, more rags now than clothing and me who dressed as if I was stepping out on the Boulevard St. Michel much to the displeasure of . . . holding on to my pants like a school boy sent home from school and set upon . . . holding them up against their eyes, against their looks, against their knowing they were going home to fuck the wife and I . . . *to see my shame*, you must not let anyone see your shame—whose voice could that be? There was never shame in my life. I have nothing to lower my head in front of. It is difficult, it hurts to raise . . .

There are grey hairs woven into the rope about my wrists. Woven by forces other than rope makers in the mountains. Of course there will be others after me but already they have scraped the hair from my wrists, from my arms, from my back, from my chest, from my head . . . one hair at a time

In Sofia Central Prison
Is there weather anymore? Will the sun come up? Will there be a sunset? Is rain expected? Has the snow finally left the . . . the jokes about the Englishman traveling through the country and being surprised when he had to be rescued from a mob wanting to stone him to death . . . seems he was trying to sell these high rubber boots, called them Wellingtons . . . it had to be explained to him, poor Englishman, the people were thinking he was insulting them . . . that he wanted them to fuck the sheep like he so obviously did, since he wore such boots and was trying . . . a very strange man . . . at least our Russian friends make no such mistakes . . . that is, mistakes that can be turned into humor . . . a humor to be kept from the ears of women, it is true . . . though all the ears of women I know, are far more experienced than . . . no man will believe this . . . I am no longer a man. I am meat waiting to be eaten by the quicklime about to be spread upon my face . . .

My first impression of Petkov was not altogether favorable. Though his shoulders were broad and his body seemed strong, he had suffered from various maladies in consequence of which he walked with an awkward limp, slouch, and his hands frequently trembled. His manner was so diffident that his circle of friends was restricted. When he spoke, he invariably looked down to avoid the eyes of his company. This young aristocrat obviously lacked the common touch that his brother Perko had possessed, and it also seemed to me that he lacked the will and courage of his brother. In this estimate, as events have proved, I was completely mistaken.

The limp posture, the trembling hands, the downcast eyes, con-
cealed a spirit as courageous and uncompromising as Petko Petkov
at his greatest.

In Paris there were no executions on view to fix in mind when I was
there. Locked away behind walls, only the notice being tacked to the
prison gate. The duty done, the deed ended. The cross shall grow roots
and fill up . . . I did not have time for those childish rhymes. My father's
face exploded. My brother's face exploded. At least they didn't shoot
them in the back . . . cancel the *them* . . . at least they did not shoot him
in the back . . . and at least they did not shoot him in the back . . . in
both cases the eyes were shattered.

To think of Basil the Bulgar Killer.
To think of the heap of eyes.
The heart of the Tsar.
The flies eating at the wounds

I would have him standing over there in the corner where they keep the
buckets. The stool is in his left hand. He would be looking at me. He is
not afraid to see what he has done. He has no private train to retire to.
No fine linen will cradle his head. His look is all he has. His eyes do not
let go. They are doing a priest's work of transubstantiation . . . this flesh
and blood, always to remain as such . . . now to be just dust in the
corner behind where he is standing . . .

Piko, Piko, Piko is that enough repetition of your name, your foolish
name, a name people in other countries will think has some sort of folk
meaning. Can you not see them calling in those experts in folk matters
to decipher your name from the bark of trees, from the shape of clouds
as they are pricked by the tops of the Rhodopes?

Piko, alas for you, poor man, with nothing to tell your grandchildren, nothing to recount, nothing to turn to singsong, nothing to bore them with so they will say, Grandpa, not again the campaign, not again that man with the knife about your throat who ended up with the knife in his stomach crying out to Allah or his mother . . . this for the little boys, while the girls turn away with: icky, icky. Nothing to tell them, nothing to pass along. You are dead before I am dead. Your mouth is frozen, your throat stopped up with: how did I . . . we all know how to complete that one, now, don't we?

Piko, why so glum? Surely you're gonna talk . . . always so talkative about the peculiarities of the last moments: the man who dared God to open his arms and spit, spit for all you are worth, worthless piece of shit that I am.

I will not offer you bail. You aren't a gypsy bear on the lead standing in the middle of Yordan Lutibrodski with young girl eyes remembering so she will recall . . . no, you are no bear. You are a man.

Just a man.

As Gosho was fond of saying, a hungry chicken dreams of millet or is it corn or is it worms or is it? There in the high chamber: where the representatives of his power sit, he will drag in the farmyard and place me upon the stool since kicked from . . . no, Piko, you did not kick it and I lifted one leg so it was easier . . . with no beard to ask you to spare . . . to be accused of allowing foreign infiltration even in here.

They will take you and make an example of you . . .

They have prepared a house for you in that amount of land sufficient, as Tolstoi urged. Will allow you the chance to grab hold of it before your time is up. How lucky you are! What won't they say back home in the village!

Just a closing off, a blocking, a getting in the way. His mouth is moving
. . . the motion of turning the tables. I am the problem. If only I had not
been alone I would not have had to die. If only they did not remember
me for whatever reason . . . and all of their reasons are compromised, I
am sure of that . . . those men who would need a map and a guide to
even find this country . . . who have to be reminded that Bulgaria is in
Europe and not in Asia or Africa . . . no, they usually get that right.
Bulgaria is not in Africa. Bulgarians are not Negroes . . . though . . .
could just as well be . . . "you ain't even a nigger" . . . is that what an
Englishman once told me? Ain't even a nigger, if you were, we would
know what to think . . .

*My interest in this far away country comes, goes. This cannot be said
for you, of you: dangling there, as it were, as it was, as it is, as . . .
waiting*

*Of course once every six months or so one of our newspapers sends a
journalist to report on the well-swept streets of Sofia.*

*We would need a major earthquake to rivet our attention, our cold eye
upon Bulgaria. I am being idealistic. The quake would have to kill in
the thousands but even then mention might not make it into two con-
secutive nights' news. So much happens, don't you know.*

Mapmakers are a busy lot. Map readers are almost non-existent.

    Petkov. "I left the Fatherland Front Government because you
started a Fascist terror. You started killing people with good
Resistance records. *As many murders lie on your conscience as on
the conscience of the greatest Fascist oppressors.*"
    Yugov. "Nikola Petkov has taken part in conspiracies."

At this point the Secretary-General of the National Committee
of the Fatherland Front, Madame Tsola Dragoycheva, member of
the Communist Party Executive, and a heroic partisan leader
during the Resistance, interjects angrily:
"Petkov is a thousand times traitor."
Someone from the Opposition bench replies:
"His brother was also accused of being a traitor and shot,
but . . ."
Nikola Petkov himself rises to his feet, and facing the Communist majority, says:
"*I am not afraid of the bullet.*"
This is clearly too much for Yugov. He must have had in mind,
even at that time, December, 1946, the sort of end his henchmen
were preparing for Petkov in the following September. So amidst
loud cheers from the Communists he roars at Petkov the following
sarcastic comment:
"*We shall not waste a bullet on you.*"
As though to give more credence and more authority to this new
constitutional warning on the part of his Police Minister, Georgi
Dimitrov gives him a hand, and adds:
"*It would be a pity for the bullet!*"
The parliamentary stenographer reports that this very witty, or
perhaps I should say, this utterly democratic remark of Comrade
Dimitrov was greeted with even "louder cheers" from the Com-
munist benches. Petkov replied:
"It's so clear, isn't it, that all this is leading to my physical
extermination? Well, hurry up and get it over! Why all the delay?"

A man is sitting in a large wooden wheelchair on the corner of Boulevard
St. Michel. He has an eagle chained to the arm of the chair. A friend
said the man was Swedish which I find, found, hard to believe. The
people of the North, from my experience, hide away all remnants of
what they . . . allow hesitation. That man with the eagle chained to the
arm of his wheelchair . . . I should begin an anecdote, though the time is
passed for such . . . now they are scraping the flesh from the hide of the
bear to place it in the rebuilt apartment of Yavarov . . . remembering

eagles like swans, like crows, mate for life and when the partner dies, is taken from them . . . I leave no one.

I first met Nikola Petkov in Paris in 1930. The opposition in Bulgaria was preparing to make a bid for power, and we were anxious to have him join us. Petkov at that time was leading the life of a young aristocrat and had no profound interest in politics.

WHAT. WHAT. WHAT.

Could have been a mad woman, though dressed for the night. something had happened. She had . . .
I do not know.
Posterity I am stuck with. It is a lousy fuck.

Dead. Dead. Dead.

Said to sharpen the mind, bring into focus with no need of elaborate theories of lenses, perspective.
Not true. The same muddle. The same hopes. Needless to worry, though. It is almost done with. No wall is going to crack open. No angel is gonna appear. I never believed in angels. If angels had not alone been on the lips of *babas* and men with a boot in the grave and the other pledged; always the chance . . .

He kept hitting me. My mouth was swollen shut, my nose, my ears, my throat, they had kicked *there* so many times I wished to be a mule . . .   bullshit, beyond wishes, beyond . . .

I am always polite. My manners keep people just where they are supposed to be. It has never been my intention to be mean to any one

person. I have not sought out their company. There must be a reason for
this . . . why should I care now? I have no cares, only this slow
dying . . . as if life were not a slow death . . . or a slow confirmation of
the moment of our birth,

A person is introduced to me. I extend my hand as is only proper. I say
hello. I do not say one more word. That is the obligation of the person
introduced to me. He says something; I say in reply, is that so . . . they
go away.

You must never jump into a conversation. People are waiting with their
moments to load upon your shoulders. Narrow shoulders have become
a modern epidemic. There is a constant effort to shed . . . to place and
just because of the blood of my brother, the blood of my father on the
paving blocks, it is assumed I have grown calluses on my shoulders.

One never knows
until it's too late
never
yet, it wasn't my failure to understand
            or my failure to see through
            or my failure to remember
            rather
I should have kept saying to myself:

    The Agrarian Movement is composed of wings, winglets and
    feathers—

I too was blinded by the truth of the statement. Oh, how we are blind when we know the truth. In this knowing comes an awful contempt—a saying of what can you expect, leading to: they deserved it all and so, Piko, kind, kicks the stool

(Piko is heard to say, I did not kick, even you have said so . . . a memory going . . . my memory going but you did say . . .)

It might have been possible to stay in my room among the French who will never admit I am here. It is not in their nature to acknowledge the presence of a foreigner in their midst.
It was impossible for me to go to America. We Bulgarians do not take easily to the passage across waters. We are rooted to mountains. There is not that itch to go rooted in the flesh of some peoples.

Oh, all this talk of peoples, nations, families . . . blood splattered on the wall . . . as addictive as human flesh to a cannibal

There was nothing to say. There was no one to say it to. None of this was my fault and yes, it was all my own fault. I should have . . . but I didn't know I should have.

The skin pricks. Ants crawl across the bottom of the window frame. Piko is looking away. He has seen it all and again. I am no different from the rest. It is just a matter of time. No one lives to tell the tale. Ain't that a kick in the head? as Ratcho would say. Ain't that a kick in the balls and him with no balls should know what he is talking about. Ain't that what someone else said?

Paris calls.
Such nonsense. A city with a mouth, with a . . . the pathetic fallacy of
some such.

Room with a high-backed stuffed chair, watching the rain come down
and the sudden appearance of an old man and woman trying to cross the
street. He holds the umbrella, she his arm. They are both getting wet.
The light from the street bursts into my eyes. I am seeing Vitosha and
Ivan falling on the path just before the summit. I did not push him. He
just fell and was crying and he old for his seven or eight years. I am ten. I
am old for my age. I have been given much and much is expected of me.
This is always being said. I let them say it.

In Paris there are few Bulgarians and they live in distant districts. I am
invited for Easter; I am invited for my name day. I am invited again and
again. I do not go out. I have much to do. I have much to catch up,
within myself.

There is no human stink to these words. You would think I was all mind,
all spirit, all words, all that stuff   long knocked out of me, I can assure
you.

Not so fast.

No way back now.
Finally to have achieved that condition . . . always before, everything I
did was compromised with the reservation *this doesn't really
matter*
            if I wanted to, I could be doing something else.
A marvelous concentration, as an Englishman might say.

Dimitrov was saved by a poem
                by a novel
                by a play played across all the stages of Europe and
even beyond, even beyond.
Not so with me. I had the people, the people. I was not born to be a
priest. I had not the knack of seeing flesh in bread or blood in wine. I
was not born into a military family. My dreams do not march and fling
me from mountain peak to mountain peak. I cannot bear to look into the
eyes of children being told their father died for . . . what is the lie being
used as I, as I . . . the people, the future . . . for the working class.
Where is the working class?
Ah, Piko, do you know where the working class is?

Gosho, Gosho . . . home, where is your home? They took you back to
the home of the working class to work on your heart and on your way
back to . . . there must be some part of the human anatomy to affix to
this country, Bulgaria. Will come to that, don't worry, there is an
epigram in the making, an epigram is aborning . . . heart repaired they
flew you back   your great heart gave out when the plane's cabin lost
its pressure.

Gosho, Georgi Dimitrov, Lion of Leipzig, Secretary of the Comintern, Bulgarian citizen, Russian citizen, Bulgarian, the boss in Bulgaria until his death in 1949.

They killed you, Gosho . . . or had you been dead for so long, so long
wanting companions in the earth that your hand continued to sign those
orders . . . come, come, join me I am lonely.

"I am confident that at the first free election this House would have a

majority made up of the elite of the Bulgarian peasantry and the elite of
the Bulgarian working class."

Did I also go on to talk about their energy
                              discipline
                              daring
                              audacity.

My rope   Tender rope   saves me from memoir writing, saves
me from grand ideas written on linen tablecloths.

Drawn back to this country by SKARA   BIERA   kebabchita
the charcoaled the seared chopped meat   tomato paste and onions
the little shop with its oven   sitting with aluminum fork, every tong
bent at a different angle, pressing them against the soiled wood table-
top to even them up a little   lift kebabchita—glory in the casual
relationship to a turd   in shape   the charred exterior, the juicy
interior
bottle of beer in hand   mouth full of beer   gulp another and then the
low burp
now, the kebabchita are delivered on large aluminum trays from the
central kebabchita factory . . carried into the shop by a blue-smocked
woman, they are counted . . . skinned rodens   sometimes they don't
get delivered and the shop offers frankfurters . . . which only the
hungry, no, the starving would eat

Discover a pattern or impose a pattern though how to avoid having to
line some up against the wall. No blood on my hands. I am sure of that. I

have signed no death warrants. At least, my conscience is clear on that ground. No one has been pushed at my suggestion. No one has suddenly found . . .

There have always been those who do not, will not fit or be fitted into their place.
Everybody has a place.

In the German cemetery near the meat packing plant, in winter, each headstone has its own clump of snow. Once, each one of those, down there, was loved or at least . . . by someone else . . . now

Suspended above a puddle of my own water. Saying I am going to sail a ship:

> remember
> when I wrote
> you:
> her eyes: blue seas
> across which I'd sail
> ships
> all burnt up

---

9 September 1944. The Fatherland Front seizes power in Bulgaria.

Only the blind see should have been the maxim of my life.

I did not even trust my guts, the palm of my hand, my twitches, the soles of my feet, the itch in my crotch. For the one good reason: living those years in Paris. I will not go on. I had thought so much I was stupid. Can one say that? Am I giving too much away? I have given everything away.

So inconsiderate. How could you have been? Didn't you learn manners as a young gentleman? Learn to have respect? Learn to be polite with all those hands waving in front of your mouth to be kissed by those plump lips? To open the door for your mother, did you not, so she could fuck every Gypsy Jew in the city of Sofia, dying didn't she of syphilis, after you had opened the door? Ah, the slanders.

You have caused us so much pain. Our fists bruised, our suppers ruined, our ears broken by the noises you have made, our suppers ruined and how many nights are we going to have to listen to the kids complain about cold food, again, and after all the time it takes to shop, not a single word from you, not a single word, is that how you are seeking to get your revenge; it little matters   we have already written out your statement, no one will say anything against it, it is already done, who cares if some urine drinker in London will say you could not have written it   do you think the world is made up of literary critics
. . . people fall asleep after the first sentence . . .

Too many things not to talk about, to admit to what I did in Paris—or to flaunt it would shake me from my moment of fame and gather me into disrepute among my valiant cow-fuckers. How false that sentiment is. I do not think of her in that way or even in the more appropriate manner.

I did not have time for that.
All those words that have to be said.
And said.
And once in a while you *do* have to listen but I was not listening then or
now.
My ears are raw with all the words . . .

She was old and had been famous when she was young for the number
of suitors, as they were called, who left gold coins on the table next to
the place of the reason why they came to call.
Oh, there were so many men, then . . . what meat was fed to the worms!
They were flung to the winds of Serbia, of Greece, of Turkey . . . how
many vain fronts swallowed them, those men who dropped gold coins?

She was thought to cry a tear for those who did not drop the coins.

I turn the page and it is blank.
Yes, really blank.
I wanted to
I hoped that
Petkov did not appear that day. Only his name was in my mouth. A
name. A foreign name but no more foreign than that ancestor who
arrived in what was to be this country with the name Nathaniel
Kidney or that baby being held by the man who is identified as my
father taking that baby from the hospital in 1944 . . .

Like dogs worrying bones in the backyard. A once a month treat of
half a cow leg for Major . . . as the month wore on would darken . . .

*the ants would move in . . . the dog would get tired of it, but didn't
know what to do with it. He didn't bury bones. He wasn't that sort of
dog . . .*
So can I drag Patchogue into this thought of Petkov.
What about Melinda . . .
*And those few friends are saying, we have heard all this before and so
have all those who have read your writings.*
Where is your discipline?
Who wants to know . . . and so forth—
*They opened the book and thinking this was going to be a long excur-
sion down memory lane, Bulgaria section, suddenly run into a little
village on Long Island and you drag in Thoreau since he had been
there years before and you might as well have a reproduction of a
painting by Philip Evergood to let people know you know that he had
been there   and just over a way Troy Donohue was sleeping on the
beach as a problem kid.*

Hey Nikola!!!!!!! I was almost two when you died, was killed.

Am thinking about Basil the Bulgar Killer, as he was known.
*As he was jokingly referred to and not a single Bulgar has ever said it
is in bad taste to say something like that.*
The year 1014.
*The Battle of Belassitza Mountain. Basil finally catches up with the
Bulgarian army of Samuel. 15,000 Bulgarians are made prisoner.
Basil orders the eyes of all of them put out save for a single eye in the
leader of every one hundred men, so that he might lead them back to
the Bulgarian king.*
*Tsar Samuel fell senseless to the ground when he saw his army and
died on September 15, 1014.*

Has a modern leader ever died when told of . . .
*Has a modern leader ever seen the handiwork of his army, walked
in . . . that small mountain of eye matter*

he who falls for his country's freedom he never dies

— **Botev**

In 1877 Dimitar Petkov, the father of Nikola P., lost an arm at the Battle of Shipka.

How to get all this history straight and not run myself into the ground.
Might as well start with the fact: Bulgaria is in the Balkans. Got that?
All you need to know . . . of course where are the Balkans . . . one stop
after Venice or one hour into your one-in-the-morning 1930s English
spy movie . . . but that's the way the wise guys have of giving you the
scoop. The other guy slides up saying, when in the Balkans you got to
be arbitrary and prepared to duck. In my case I got Bulgaria, and all
of history is seen from that hard luck, up shit's river, going down for
the third and maybe just maybe . . . no, she turns and spits you out all
over the satin sheets or he says I ain't going down on you with you on
the rag . . . and she saying . . . it's red ain't it and you said you're a
communist and off with your head . . . though you ain't got one,
anymore.

Piko has his back to me. He's filling up a bucket of water. Life goes on.
If only I had not . . . If only . . . If I . . . If . . . I . . .

Gemeto will live to be an old man rubbing up against my memory. Each
year the speech will acquire a bit more rust. Each year those listening
will be fewer in number: their hearing aids will get larger. He will need a
loudspeaker and before long

Piko knows the rest of *that* song

No way out from under the mistake. Once made, and it was not just taking a wrong street and having to backtrack a couple of hundred feet . . .

But I was a human being. I could have left at any time. There was still the apartment in Paris. No one would have cared, on that street, if I had suddenly turned up, again. The times, they would have said, the times and how lucky to have you back, the luck you must have when all we read in the papers or at least all our eyes glance over in the papers, are of walls and men crumbling in front of those walls . . .

Though the mistake was made, I could have . . . until, until, until . . .

Should I talk about the famous writing on the wall and not being able to read *that* language.

Nikola P. is born in 1892

I've talked not enough of beauty, but of what use is that where I am? Better to picture stumped men just back from the wars, those with half a head, with hair not grown back looking at the world gone mad with not believing they are going to die

die

die . . .

One of those winters in the 1930s in Venice. I spoke only French and did not betray myself to anyone. The politics were all so complicated and I . . . walking in a close passageway with goods vomited up in heaps under lighted candles I was suddenly ambushed, how else, by the harsh consonants of my language. I turned and brown eyes met brown eyes. I looked away. A head moved, and then a hand was turning a shoulder to look . . . and I ran . . . that is how they write it . . . I ran . . . no, walked quickly into the shadows . . . how lucky to be in Venice with the shadows that exist in spite of all the bad poetry written about it and to be written about shadow and stone. My heart surely a stone. You might say. To turn away from my country.

So it is reported in the American magazines that "the hooked-nosed" Bulgarian is dead.
How could they single out my nose? And in such a crude manner? A nose is the instrument of personality marshalling the force of age across the map of the face.
Six years of war leave traces in the vocabulary. Rather war than the socialist construction of the new man   to be changed to the construction of the new person in honor of the year of the woman

Her mother sends me photographs of her daughter's children. I am swallowed up in my own death. Once, yes, of cour. ., it was once . . . upon a time . . . dumber, trees, river, but to get out of the heat we went into the ossary of Rilski Monastery and the heaped-up skulls laughed at us

The deal was done. No consolation in being right with the earth filling my mouth.
Will the earth always fill up my mouth?
Well, the earth always does fill up the mouth.

And I am no different. Bloated tongue closing up against the last two teeth. They were so kind. All the others bashed out or pulled, broken off with rusty pliers. Just broken off and the bottom of my tongue raw from the saw bits of tooth remaining in jaw.

> Dimitar Petkov is murdered in February, 1907 walking in Blvd. Alexander II, Sofia.

Is anyone interested in anything?
Is it the only question worth asking . . . well, we all know the answer to that one.
Your interest ends at your mortality, at your death . . . you don't have enough time to worry about, to be part of . . .

Drive in the nails.
No, they did not puncture my flesh. I was not to receive a military death. Rather the death of a coward, the death of . . . an animal caught in a trap meant to pay back for all the efforts, wasted in trying to talk me down from the wood.

Obscurity not to protect but to

In Venice, after being disturbed, I went to the cemetery on San Michele. My fellow countrymen and women would not follow me there. They are of a more practical bent. There was nothing to buy or sell. I walked among the stacked-up stone boxes. Found myself, as if writing on a viewcard, in the foreign section in a grove of trees midst English names that would not be departing back to the green fields.

I have never been to England. Have only heard of the men in their clubs one upon the other and of the women who copulate with dogs. They are said to be a people with a cold sense of humor.

My eyes close. No, I do not see visions. I do not see. Isn't that why one closes one's eyes? To have them closed. Finally.

Okay, eyes closed and am standing on the roof of a house in Turnovo. My father is arguing and his voice suddenly stops. The silence is answered by silence.

His voice begins again only lower this time. With two sons my life is not without hope.

How many bullets are there in a revolver? Your two sons are so few.

Piko is pissing in the bucket he has emptied across the floor. How can he do that . . . of course he had been out the night before, actual time . . . in the middle of the night now and so all afternoon he must have been in the shops putting away the raki . . . Piko is a raki man.
He will be done with me and the table waits for him to claim his place and he will fall silent. I give myself, as usual too much dignity, too much respect.

Or in Beograd, in the old city, near the Kalemegdan fortress looking down to the Sava I turned, and saw her standing, her hair burst in sunlight. She was from Finland, she later said, while we drank slivovitz.

Burst into light and her blue eyes held my heart, the street juggler just
before he heaves the balls into the air . . . how sentimental, how phony,
how false, how like a young man who does not yet,   but even that
would be false; I knew life was . . . here I go again, here he goes again,
get out the bench and line up the doddering old men in the sunlight, their
hands gnarled over their sticks standing in the mud between their bowed
legs . . . life is a terminal illness . . . but would never say or print it out
for the public eye.

I claim no hidden life. I am a name in the history books. I am a man in
the accounts of

A taste for champagne is acquired. Must say this for Gosho   when
we were in Moscow, he knew I had been in Paris and there on the table,
from France . . . and not just one or two bottles . . . but bottle after
bottle and the next morning they could have scraped the floor off the
roof of my mouth. Gosho was always a large man. The backseat of a
limousine suited him. For some reason he liked to have women drivers.
He did not use them for any other purpose. I know. I know there was
talk. Gosho was married to a book and all his juices flowed out of his
eyes and into the pages. I think he envied Hitler and the tall men about
him, all with blonde hair. That is only a passing thought. It could be true
or it could be a story that moved from café to café.

On October 23, 1944, Nikola P. is in Moscow to be one of the
signatures on the armistice.

Piko, if he spoke and he does, he is not a mute, in spite of what some
might think, begins, I can hear him, I who have the gift to . . . no gifts,
his voice sitting behind a desk, the light grey in the room, he has been up
all night, should I say I had to see him in a provincial city in France, to
see him in Bulgaria would make him a laughingstock, he is saying, all I
have is contempt for these men in politics, for these politics, he takes a
sip of sweet wine, it is late at night, the good wine is long gone and it is
still hours before the light comes back, contempt, if only I could drain
that word of any sense of taking an interest in, because to say contempt
is to say I have, had given a certain amount of thought . . . which is true
but it is more to avoid just the shrug of the shoulder . . . I do have some
matter between my ears, bats are not circulating in that region

Niko Niki Niki . . . you could have
lived out your life with your country safely far away . . . but now you
have to live with the choruses singing that you gave your life in the
cause of freedom, in the cause of your country, in . . . when all you did
was have the life squeezed out of you, a sack of guts about to burst

Dado built this prison. As a child we walked through the construction.
He looked to Europe. There was hope in every man. There was no need
to turn a man into an animal. To reduce a man. Yes, to punish but also
to lead, to show, to help. They cased up his sentiments in cement and
made walls of them.

*Ten leva and he would suck my cock for me. Pay me in hard cash for
my hard cock in his mouth. And I just wanted to piss and get back to
the latest news. It only happened one time to me in The Bambouk. He
made his offer and I refused his offer. I see him on the streets after. He
does not recognize my face. I don't think he cared about my face. He
had grey eyes and thin lips. A tuft of hair came out of his ear.*

Later, Colonel S. W. Bailey, who had driven G. M. Dimitrov through the Soviet cordon to Barnes' villa, reported on the girl's injuries to the Foreign Office:

> I am informed by the doctor, who was in attendance on the girl's mother when the coffin was opened, that the following injuries—difficult to explain by the effect of a fall even from a fourth floor window—were established, in addition to the bullet and knife wounds.
> 1. All the nails on both feet had been torn out.
> 2. Three fingers of the left hand had been hacked off at the second joint.
> 3. Both ears cut off.
> 4. Right breast excised.
> 5. Tongue torn out and all teeth extracted.
> 6. Flaying of a strip of skin about two inches wide through one quadrant of the waist.
>
> Demands for the preparation of a protocol setting out these facts were, somewhat understandably, refused.

On May 30 Barnes communicated to Washington his information on Mara Racheva's condition at death, which generally coincided with that provided by Colonel Bailey. Foreign observers agreed that she had died under torture in the depths of the central police station.

In 1904, D. Petkov, the father of N. Petkov, ordered work begun on a new modern central prison in Sofia.

Anha wrinkled so deep no powder would cover the years. He does not exaggerate. He has always been careful not to insult the old; always careful to avoid summing them up into their shaking limbs, a wandering mind stuck with too many qualifications . . . that is all the years bring:

qualifications.
No longer the hotness, the coldness . . . now everything is temperate.
No glance,
no phrase,
no

But Anha would have none of this.
Niki, she would say, what are you doing wasting your time with an old
woman? You must be out there . . . and even that is such ordinary
advice.
What is out there?
Anha looks away. What else is she supposed to do? She is caught
in:::::could hear the violins, the clouds being cranked into place.

> Mara Racheva was secretary to N. Petkov.

Blood, blood, blood. The dreariness of the whole business. We have to
get out the tin basins, fill them with blood and "have a good wash," as
the English say.

succeeded in imitating it, although many people had tried. The
one-two jerk, he was told (to his surprise—which he shrewdly did
not show) was the only thing that could prevent the extrusion of the
tongue, which otherwise would blossom out into a repulsive blue
flower.

No one to turn to.
Plug pulled.
Switch switched.
Door closed.

Your man is saying, didn't you figure out that your days were numbered though you were probably one of those snobs that didn't go to the movies? Even a kid, I would think, could have figured it out when the judge decided to dish out 100 corpses instead of the expected 50 or so; had them lined up against the wall 20 at a time, even a kid and you an adult back from Paris, from London, from Moscow . . . surely, you weren't ain't a sod buster from the sticks suddenly finding himself having to have clean fingernails . . .

June 14, 1924, Petko D. Petkov, the brother of Nikola, is gunned down near the Narodnia Sobranie.

So or should come up with made-up speeches for my man. Face the fact of tedium and stuff some rotting newspaper down your throat to give you a feel of the public words of this man.
However.
I have enough respect for you, for myself. I cannot read that earnest rubbish. One Gettysburg Address is enough and where is that silver star won for memorizing it though not a gold because the recital lacked pizzazz?

A gist of the speech, allow me, would be:
them and us
their and our   and for the longest
time I went on with how it was possible, could be possible to avoid
conflict or if there was a conflict there was no need for gentlemen to
gnaw at each other's throat.

Should have realized, but too late. Them and Their were always
capital lettered words.

It was a sunny day in Sofia, Bulgaria. Nikola, Niki to his friends, was a happy man even though he was going to be hanged that evening in a prison his father had built forty years before . . .

His man is saying, what to make of this dude: he spoke his own Bulgarian, Russian, French, English with an accent to be sure, some German, a smattering of Italian and it's said by some he could even understand the Jewish in their synagogue down there on Ulitza George Washington. I have my doubts about this and know what people are getting at when they say he could speak Jewish. Not that any of us . . . didn't even Tsar Boris tell Hitler he couldn't have any of *his* Jews? But it's knowing all these languages. You'd think in one of them it would get through his skull: there were people who didn't wish him a long life.

Piko has cleaned out his bucket, filled it. He has coiled up the spare rope, the blistered hose, put away the ladder. He's the orderly sort. If you get too far behind in your daily chores, on this job, there's no telling what can happen.

September, 1967. Thomas McGonigle arrives in Sofia. On Hristo
Botev Boulevard he meets Lilia Ratcheva Vassileva. They marry
and leave for Venice and Dublin in April of 1968.

*Proverbial party at which no one comes, to mistranslate from some
language, to provide a snigger in the back row. Must always do that.
They don't want to be here. Can't say I blame them. I had no choice in
the matter. I just got off a train and was really on my way to somewhere else. Thought it not good form to just pass through a country
and anyway a stop in Bulgaria was something to write home to the
folks about. Can't say I blame a single one of them. I too would have
my doubts. No throat grabbed, to be vulgar about it, lowering the
value of all which has come and gone before. No relative of the person
met and married and now living out a friendship, onto the grave, onto
the grave. After so many years and no longer intimate, there is very
little can happen between two people to drive in an unbridgeable
chasm of doubt. Enough of that in the past, if I or she, who is much less
likely, cared to dredge up... vast machines are necessary for
dredging and then those long huge pipes rusting for most of the year in
the yard down by the Patchogue River, to carry the sand to the beach
from the river bottom... getting too confused... a party and no one
came. Not for want of trying at that one party at least the center attraction would come, or try to come, though his body by now has long been
drained of all fluids. He is beyond even sweating. He sweats but no
water comes to his brow or between his shoulder blades.*

A stab into the charted, oh, so charted wastes of the modern mind.

*Have me, your man, getting off the train. September. As good as any
month in the year. Not even having to force the monthly anniversary of
9 September, or 23 September, or... what day was it, around five
o'clock in the afternoon. Her mother had gone to take a shit and she
was filling in at the kiosk, just back from school, still in her school*

uniform, wearing a blue sweater because the black jumper did not
keep her warm enough, she always feels the cold . . .

If I could tell you why. If I could find the words. How many times has
that been said? At least repeating words sanctified and not worn out by
use. There must be a heart somewhere in the midst of them. Is that
possible, still . . . in this day of the age. No, go on sit them all about the
table and get the news of the day over with.
It was a wonderful day.
We all went out and all came back.
We are all going to sleep and are all going to wake up.
That is the hope.
We have all gone out for the day and all come back from the day and
now it is night and we have heard there was a hanging and we are all
glad it was not anyone any of us knew, personally, that is, speaking out
of concern for the necessary tears to be shed and the printing of notices
to show our death to the world.
We do not hide away our deaths.
We advertise them like orange juice, now available, as are apples
coming all the way from America, imagine apples and next year there is
talk of pears coming all the way from America. How do they come that
far? Why do they come that far?

In the shops they are selling peppers from Bulgaria and cheese from
Bulgaria; that is all.

I feel this. I feel that. I this other.
You feel this. You feel that. You feel.
All this awful feeling.
An epidemic of feeling.
Not a drop of meaning in any of it. Just wind passing over the teeth.

Misdirected assbreath.

We had gone to Vienna and they watched us. Glasses fell from our hands, newspapers would not fold in the expected manner. Farts, sneezes, coughs all at the wrong time flew from our bodies. Pursued through the streets he and I thought, with the curse: gardener, gardener out of the parlour with those mud splattering boots!

We thought. Their voices never let up. They watched us all the time and counted in their eyes the miles to Vienna from whence we had come and back, back you all must go. Maybe another year, when you have . . . maybe another year, another century.

We were as modern as the next . . . citizens of a country complete with German king.

Incest, fratricide, matricide, patricide—keep it in the family. The smallness of the place. Eventually the borders close down to four by six by six.

> . . . while working on my book on the
> facial play of the insane
> —Ernst Juenger

We are five people: *Medy* Trufana
                      Lilia Ratcheva
                      Toshko Todor

Ruth
Thomas
We are in the apartment of Lilia in New York City. A Thursday night in the summer.
Medy sits on the rollaway bed made into a backless sofa. Toshko sits on the same bed but leaning into the corner made by the two walls.
Lilia sits on a pillow in front of the record player.
Ruth sits on a pillow in the corner opposite Toshko, though not exactly in the corner because there is a cloth chair and book-shelves in the corner.
Thomas sits on the floor, next to Ruth and in turn next to Medy.
Food is spread out on platters on the floor: shrimp grilled in their
shells
kefta kabob
grilled green peppers
shredded red cabbage
green salad
large round loaf of home-
made bread with knife
punctures in crust.
A bunch of flowers from the Korean store on the corner of Christopher Street.
A litre bottle of wine ... glasses, silverware, plates, napkins ...
Medy does not speak English beyond thank you and maybe one or two other phrases. Thomas and Ruth do not really speak Bulgarian. Thomas knows some words, some phrases; he can ask simple questions, he can count. He at one time thought he could figure out what people were saying. He was usually wrong. Bulgarian is a harsh sounding language with many hard consonants giving the impression of being a language that conducts conversation as a verbal brawl.
Lilia is Medy's daughter.
Toshko is the nephew. His mother lives in Australia.
It, the reason for the people and the food being in this room, is that it's Medy's birthday. Hanging across the archway that separates the two rooms:
CHESDITA ROSHDEN DEN MEDY
All this is place setting.
Get to the job of work. I am going to interview Medy. She is

reluctant and I am dependent on Toshko and Lilia. I have been married to Lilia for 15 years. I have lived with Ruth for 5 years. Toshko is more agreeable. Lilia shares her mother's disinterest in politics, in anything that is *serious*. She puts up with and lets everybody know that she is putting up with it. Ruth says a couple of times that enough's enough. She is from the outside though she has known these people for five years. She has only known the more agreeable sides of all of them. She has not seen knives pulled, blows exchanged, words thrown about like   fill in any word that seems to fit.

I had prepared questions on lined paper, leaving space for answers. Eventually I felt a bit stupid. I kept on. I enjoyed feeling almost silly, just this side of silly. I was conscious of what I was doing: find material for this Petkov book...

How old are you?   71.

                  Not a wrinkle, Lilia says, pointing to her mother's face. Lilia says her dermatologist says, soap and water, that's the secret. 71. Lilia is eating tomatoes because they are good for the skin. They can't find good tomatoes here. In Bulgaria tomatoes are so plentiful you get sick of them, real tomatoes...

Where were you born?   Strashitza in the district of Turnovo. You always say that. So people know where you are from. A lot of villages, selos.

What did your father do?   A farmer.

And your mother?   Same. She is 95 and still living in the village.

How many brothers and sisters?   One brother and one sister. The Brother Ivan is dead. Heart condition. *Nema kizmet*, as is always said after his name. He was not allowed to get married. The sister is married and lives in Sofia. She had lived in Budapest and was a gardener. She is the mother of Ginka who lives in Brooklyn, whose daughter married a man who owns a pizza parlour: Dede is a subject of much *nema kizmet* though what can you expect with a mother like Ginka.

The dinner is eaten and questions answered.

Medy went to Sofia when she was 17. Since she was/is 71 with this birthday in 1983, she was born in 1922 and went to Sofia in 1939. Lilia says we don't know how lucky we are to have escaped the shit that her mother had to wade through. Medy was married to a man from her village. He was four years older. They ran a vegetable

shop in Sofia on Ulitza Tsar Simeon. It was not in the market.
Medy's husband was from Strashitza. He also had been a gardener
in Budapest. He is now 75 and lives in the mountains outside Sofia
with his pigs and fruit trees. Medy divorced him when Lilia was a
child. He was a drunk and a beater. He didn't know his own father. I
say, that is why you Lilia... eventually the story is that he died, that
is, his father died while his wife was pregnant... or something like
that. Lilia has not seen him since she was 11 or 12 and has no wish
to see him though he is said to have a desire to see the daughter
who went to America.

Was he a soldier?   That's a personal question. The only
time Medy says this. I answer that among us, like us sitting in this
room, there is nothing personal. He was a soldier. He was a cook
and was sent to Greece some time during the war.

Did your parents have any political opinions?   Medy
keeps talking (much time has passed) about this family she knows
who do have political feelings, beliefs and who were close to
Petkov. Some people have them and other people do not. I try to
tell her I am interested in HER opinions. HER REACTIONS. She
says I should talk with these people. Lilia, Toshko and Ruth point
out that Medy was young when she left home, 17... she does not
know if her parents were in any political party. They owned land. 5
decaters of land. It is not very much.

Where were you, Medy, on 9 September 1944?   Strashitza.
There had been bombings in the winter of 1943-44 in Sofia and
they fled by train. 10 in the bathroom or something like that. They
were very afraid.

What happened on that day?   Yordan, your *kum* (god-
father at our wedding) showed up with his gun and went off to join
the partisans. He was her nephew. He is now a retired lawyer.

Medy, who was Nikola Petkov?   She does not reply. Lilia
says, Medy was taking care of her nuts.

What do the names Yugov, G.M. Dimitrov, Kostov, Kolarov mean?
Medy knows who Yugov was. A change of voice when that name is
mentioned. A comfortable fear... she knows the names from the
radio. She listened to the radio: what was said, what was not said.
She remembers hearing about Nikola Petkov on the radio; about
him being thrown out of the *Sobranie*... with Chervenkov things
were a little better... with the current Zhivkov... he was a swine-
herd and the most harmless, that's why he's there now. That's why

they had him. The communists took care of all of their own. A gesture of a knife going across the throat and a smile on Medy's face. About Petkov she remembers hearing about him on the radio but she didn't know what he did and by the time she understood something of what he did: he was dead.

Medy doesn't remember if she ever voted before 1944. After 1944 they were voting all the time but it didn't matter.

Did she ever join a party?   IT WAS a time OF MISERY.

Do you remember hearing Petkov's name in recent times?

It is not a name you say in public. Thomas, Lilia is saying, would go to Bulgaria and get himself arrested for walking up to the wrong person and asking, do you know who Petkov is? With Petkov, you only talk about such things, within the family and after the windows are closed and when you have gone to such efforts, you don't talk about such things from the past because trouble is the only consequence.

Three tall candles on the cake from Patisserie Lanciani. We are about to sing. One of the candles goes out. Toshko re-lights it with his lighter. We sing in English. Lilia explains to Medy about wishes. She blows all the candles out.

Left with a feeling of foreboding.

Always sad at birthdays. They are deathday celebrations.

Who won't be with us next year, my mother is saying. One year it does happen.

I would like to go back to Bulgaria with Medy and then meet Lilia and Ruth in Venice.

That would be a perfect holiday, some year.

Some year.

One afternoon we were talking about appropriate honesty and how there are those moments when to speak is to slip a noose around your own neck. I said, I thought then, for the sake of argument that there is never a time when honesty is not appropriate.

Gosho, it must have been or Alexander then, made a noise deep in his gullet and drew an imaginary knife across his own throat. Must have been born with brown feet or he's been tramping through shit his whole life.

An epigram as effective as a threat. Ender of conversation, a bit of wisdom I did not take to heart. I chose to annoint their threats with the phrase of heightened rhetoric. They don't really mean what they say. They are saying it only for effect, only for the newspapers, out to score points on a score card only their own members are holding... to choose and not to see, to not hear a threat once spoken never retracted. It ends all conversation... and yes, of course, it's human nature for conversation to start up again after a lull though always there is now the addition to the room, off to the side, never spoken, the threat, and poems should be written, as useful or as useless as anything to ward off...

My shit flowing down the insides of my legs.
Though I could be mistaken.
Nothing, yes erection, but nothing all beaten out, squeezed out... an erection so they say...
All this language so pretty, so careful, so refined... behind bloated tongue, behind blistered lips, broken lips, behind gums torn, eyes beaten shut, ears scuffed.

They lifted my head up with ice tongs.
Do I remember the joke.
A block of ice for your excellency.
Knees bend.
Whiskey for the gentleman, like his English bosses serve.
A whiskey drinker sits in Lenin Square in a café frequented by students from the school for the deaf and dumb. A whiskey drinker and a woman come up to him from the National Choir. They begin to talk.

Years later he remembers her. There is no way for them.

It is all a long time ago.

Everything is always a long time ago.

Gosho slept as sound as a log. No. Never had tapped out messages on the side of his skull.

Sergei is placing his hand upon my knee.
How, he is saying, I envy the young. Their flesh not wrinkled with the
passage of many hands.

We have to do more research.
We should wait and see.
We have to give names, stick them to this   that.
Every time he heard, we have to do more research, it was as if electrical impulses were sent to his fingers that typed out death sentences . . . they would have all the evidence they needed here and now.
Where did this message come from?

March 1, 1941. Nikola P. sent to a concentration camp in Bulgaria, later released.
January, 1944. Nikola P. is again sent to a camp; he is released in August, 1944.

I would sit at an architect's tilted table and write long sentences, turn to typewriter to copy what was to be read aloud in the evening.
Now I write a short sentence, that product of rush, of demands of work
          sandwiched between the projects of the vulgar . . . I would go so far as to say sandwiched between the schemes of those who do not have souls and those who will sleep through the agony of their deaths.

How I hate the short sentence, that product of rush, of work, of dead-lines, of distraction.

and this thought rushed, lost . . . not able to read the scrawl on a page left behind in the morning . . . the thought mangled with the passage of time . . . now early morning and all thought shattered—after the day.

The baskets with the sewn cloth tops would be heaped up about them as they squatted in the square. Dumadzhamas of wine placed near their wrapped legs. The wicker was tan in the bright sun. Thin straps of black mirror, almost, the worn handles.
Where is the poet? They are never around when you need them. Off in their villas complaining.

They would come up to me.
They would come up to me.
They would look at me out of the corners of their practiced eyes.
What do you know about the earth?
I'd look at them.
There would be a pause.
I do know.
They'd go away.
I do not know why. I had nothing more to say.
They had nothing more to say.

There was something almost Roman about the whole business. I let it pass.
What else was there to do?

A hot Tuesday night working in The East Side Book Shop on St. Marks Place. There is no air-conditioning. The fans are placed at angles that don't do very much except, as they say, move the hot air about . . . all sorts of hot air. Sitting at the low chair behind the table, behind the cash register, looking out at the couple of customers, browsing in the magazines, grazing midst the literature shelves. And struck
Bang.
Just like that.
Bang   struck   how very far away this man Nikola Petkov is from me . . . how far away I am   how far he is.   I saw him. I was in The Bambouk and no, you ain't about to get some out of the body mysticism, that is down there at the back of the shop on the right-hand side after women's studies, history, psychology,   beyond the pillar . . . no   STRUCK   bang   just like that.
I looked around the noted titles: wrote them down because I have a bad memory and I like lists, copying lists over again . . . names or names of photographed people, all of THIS STUFF that is accumulated . . . and in ten years, sometimes five, requires footnotes:
   Looking: Brooke Shields, John Travolta, Nicaragua, El Salvadore, Kathy Acker, Fear, Elvis Costello, Barbara Holland, October, Situationalist International, Berlin Alekanderplatz, Psychedelics Encyclopedia, Adrift, Triage, Big Time Review, Elle, Sight and Sound, L'Argent, Bodies and Souls, Kaputt, 4 Days at Shatila, The Face, Photo, Public Illumination Magazine . . .

Country and Western music on KIK: every night I cry
                                    you keep staying on my mind
                                    time's not gonna heal
                                          this wound

MUSIC   FILM   USED BOOKS   NEW BOOKS   NYC TRAVEL
large breasted black bra'd women . . . small women in white T-shirts . . . girl went to a David Bowie concert and had a religious experience . . . you got to have worshippers in order to have God . . . I don't know what comes first . . . and I believe in God . . . the David Bowie concert was a religious experience

    in the 60s the slogan on the street was "a bed for a bang" . . . it's very hot and some say the owner of the shop has cancer of the stomach or intestines . . . he's sick . . . some say he is dying . . . some say . . . a lot of some saying

and then   here I am collecting pages of the corpse dream of Nikola Petkov.   My nose stopped up for a moment with a female armpit hair.

To go back there. That was usually in my head. Back there surrounded by the smell of coal, of shit in the streets, of the shove, of the rudeness, of the waiting for someone to take offense . . . the waiting for the spark . . . no political message implied. I had no intentions of traveling to Leningrad to pay homage to a ship, to the champagne they were about to launch

ISKRA

You sometimes have no choice in the matter. You do what you have to do and then

Been in the hole longer than most of you have been alive.

Might as well stick a housing project over the space where they planted
what was left of me. Or would that be too much

heavy handed   pounding the
message into the ground   where else is one supposed to be pounded?

They knew what to do with me.

Gosho with his chicken dreams will live to have the corn growing out of
his asshole.

However, we will have to wait some time before that happens. They
have him   or what remains of him on display in that fine display case
     done up by the traveling firm that did Lenin, Stalin and later will do
Ho and Mao   waiting in the wings to do Fidel.

An earthquake would get him out of there. It has to happen one of these
days.

Even the hottest day or come to think of it the coldest day   comes to
an end   in spite of thoughts moment to moment, is this ever going to
end

everything has an end.   No one has the patience to accept this . . .

*a prose urging from forgetfulness the memory of the 12 or so strangled
minutes in the life of Nikola Petkov, last leader of the Agrarian
Movement in Bulgaria, hanged by the Lion of Leipzig, Georgi
Dimitrov, in Sofia, Bulgaria, 23 September 1947*

A deal could have been worked out, I am sure. Piko has been smirking all along. Saying with the corners of his mouth: the fool, the fool . . .
unlike the rest of us, he could have worked, done a deal as an Irishman might say, done a deal with THEM . . . not like us who don't even get a chance to . . . pick the pot the piss is going to collect in as a guy from Plovdiv might say. HIM, there, rope, there . . . when he didn't have to be . . . he could have left with Gemeto or right after to a sports car on the Riviera . . . so he would have to be a little inventive about how and why he ended up . . . but who's to know? Who even knows where this country is? Not as if, once he got wherever he ended up, he was going to run for Pope or King or President or dog catcher . . . the checks would arrive from some source and he would live. That's all that matters   to live.   Anyone can die.

So you say Piko.
So I do
Though, who is going to write about you Piko?
At least, I will not be forgotten . . . I will not have that awful fate . . . I will not turn to dust on a library shelf. Into the ground with me when I am done and let the corn grow tall out of my asshole.

Did he ever smile? It's said he enjoyed a laugh once in awhile but the times do not allow for many of those moments.

He had been too much alone. At the end, imagine it, at the end with the itch of the rope in front of his nose they were crowding about him with the hope he would place them somewhere. They didn't care where or how; just thought he would know where they were supposed to go.

Produced a laugh deep within him. It would come out. He would startle his closest friends with that laugh. They would say it was the pressure. He had to let off steam somehow and he did not give way to tantrums about people who put their feet up on desks . . . so he laughed.

Who has ever escaped getting wet when it rains?

There were no hooks, opening lines, punch lines in his memory.

So tired.
Ghost, where are you now, with my mouth smashed in? The words do
not . . .

My life will be turned over to editorial writers . . . to self-serving
politicians who will see in the recital of my name some imagined
advantage.
If only they knew.
When you got to ask: who is this man HE'S GOING ON ABOUT . . .

Gosho's mother is a knitter. The journalists came to her, to ask her what
she thought of The Petkov Trial.
Who's he?
Of his death?
What was his name?
He was one of your son's defenders.
He is my son. My son had many defenders once upon a time.
And did not Nikola help your son?
So it is said . . . who is this man and who are you?
Do you not think it ironic?
I am not a political person. My son knows best. I do not pen
philosophical works.

Each page is an urging into being . . . for the minutes of the reading of these pages of a man . . .

And the objections can be lined up . . . taken out to the courtyard and shot in batches of ten.

When you pull your head out of the sand there is a man ready to greet you, a knife in his hand waiting for your neck.

> November 1945. Telegram George returns to Bulgaria from the Soviet Union having renounced Russian citizenship and sent his two Bulgarian co-defendents from the Reichstag Fire Trial to Siberia to die.

The years leave no pattern that is of any help because we are always within the years within the pattern . . . only the sudden shock of how few years are left. Once I watched an old Turk taking off his boots before he entered the mosque. There was nothing special about the man: he was an old man who was taking off his boots. In a couple of years he would be dead. There would be another old man taking off his boots, one of those days, to be seen when walking past the mosque . . . surely it means something . . . I thought of him for a moment before rising to speak in the Sobranie . . . the thought led nowhere. He did not appear in my speech.

I have to leave it like that.
Just like that.
Would it make any difference if I made the old man into an old

woman and had her lighting a candle in *the black church*, watching her lips kiss the glass entombed ikon . . . the puckered lips . . .

They said he had been famous since he was a young man but I did not know him or his books. I was not much of a reader. I wanted life to, as the saying goes, write its novel upon my flesh, within my heart, on my face, at the tips of my fingers. I did not want to have to paw through pages of books, imagine books and French books at that . . . of a young man who   and young women who and oh, isn't it all so sad?

Gide was his name, they said after he left. He was talking about sin with a friend. I did not have anything to say. I am not blessed with religion or cursed . . . most times I think it is a curse . . . cursed, bowed down to the earth.

Pages get turned but the situation remains the same. The rope is doing its job . . . which is an insult to the truth because, as Aquinas might write, a thing of itself cannot be either good or evil . . . since it lacks a soul . . . the ability to reason . . . it can only be put to use by a person who in turn can be either good or evil in his/her action . . . am I getting this right? . . . or just digging into the flesh of Petkov knowing he had no time for religion . . . just tapping a little earth down upon his closed eyelids . . .

no, they are open. bugged out his eyes are . . . and not a thoughtful pair of hands to close them over.

Piko mutters it is not so, they just would not close.

Am I responsible for what the rope does to the human face?

I tried to travel him to Paris. I have tried to sit him at a table with Gide. They have not found much in common to talk about. Gide was not having any of this talk about separating the evil of a country from its people. Niki, much against all that history would have him believe, does not like dislike the Turks as a people. Gide dislikes their trousers . . . those trousers which make them look like they are carrying a load of shit between their legs.

Gide is interested in bulges.

Niki turns away. He is not so far away from home to have to put up . . . he knows what is coming next. He always knows what is coming next when he talks with these people: the wild mountains of your home and women dragged up mountainsides to be raped, with repeated ecstasy filling cinema screens.

There are no books in Niki's head. It is a pity. It leads to large blank spots on the map. A map is filled up with imagined worlds. Until a place is imagined between the covers of a book it can be said to not exist. Bulgaria is said to exist because of Turgenev . . . but that guy dies in Venice.

With each word written

It is not the rope, but pencils first doing the rough calculations, then the ink pens, then the typewriters, again the pencils for corrections; lastly inked confirmations of the corrections for the fine tunings of the public documents behind which it finally can be said it is a noose tied at the end of a rope fastened to an overhead beam . . .

So few will know . . .   Europe
                            The Balkans
                            Bulgaria
                            Sofia
                            Turkey
                            The Balkan Wars
                            IMRO
                            Agrarian . . .
                            The Second World War . . . now there's
where we can pick up the ears . . . that shelf dressed in SS black and GI
fatigues presided over by two gents with moustaches, a guy with leg
braces and cigarette holder . . . a wife who they say . . . and that
drunken Englishman who has been around for so long that . . .

A private life. I am sure it could be invented for a visiting journalist. Not
that I believe it is possible to have one in this day of this age. There's a
Bohemian crystal vase brought back by Gemeto: Nina could have
placed a Moreno glass flower in it and it could be talked about . . .
better to dust flowers than to have to keep replacing them . . . or does
that echo too much the boulevard?

There should be something of the common touch, but not that common,
so the impression is given, I have made a raid upon the people of the
earth and am now displaying my credentials. Leave such stunts for
Telegram George.

It could have been worse, to have done nothing, to be dying in bed,
alone, say, a room, with a single light bulb, at the end of a noose of
electric cord.
The breath of regret pressing my puckered lips.
At least to have lost, to become a creature in the theology of the victor

... all heroes, all victors require the vanquished, the defeated, the losers.
So we go hand in hand into history, Gosho.
Ain't that a kick in the head.

On August 21st I called a number given me by Iskar. I took it from the letter that the man's name was Petroff. I had tried calling a couple of times before. Today was Sunday afternoon. A man answered... hesitating between English and Bulgarian. I introduced myself as being interested in Nikola Petkov... the business about the name came up and the man said his name was Petkoff, and spelled it in the French style though in English of course you can spell it Petkov with a v. I am his nephew and am in my 70s. It is very hot and I have someone visiting. When it is cooler. I said I would write him a letter explaining my interest so when we got together...

So, for a hundred pages I have been writing about a fiction and now I am talking with the fleshy voice of a relative of that fiction.

I am sure this is a confusion of genres... an asking of what's going on... I am afraid of this turn in events... what though can any voice add to what I have imagined, already known, or drawn out from already published statements...

To have to deal with a real person. Maybe I should put real in quotation marks as in "real" person... and then I have to figure out who Niki is... this creation I have grown fond of as he dangles from the rope, as he dies... as the rope takes on a life of its own... now, this real person who is the nephew of this person I have been writing about is now going to become part of...
                    might end up as a theoretical article in

some awful art magazine

I don't want that.   *Keep in our mind that Niki is still at the*
rope's end. He is . . .

                    no closer   no further away than he was . . . this is
just   m-o-r-e i-n-f-o-r-m-a-t-i-o-n

Skin like any other man's.
Sweat like any other man's.
Blood like any other man's.
That just about sums up the case against this man, this Niki . . .
The lurch to the common, to show, we too are human: that he was
human, to turn the ritual into drama so we will know, for sure, it is
coming to an end . . . only one more commercial announcement and
then the final drop to: CREDITS.

Been going around saying, even the rope becomes a character in the
bit of prose I have been filling up my time with . . . no need really to
say that about Petkov. He did not live in a time when he had to find
things to fill up his time.
Don't worry, no deep thinking going on here.

Don't these guys get tired?
Haven't they had enough?
Maybe they didn't read Henry Miller at an early age.
Is that why Europe is now thought of as a primitive place . . .
          that remembered scene from a movie, the first American-made
film to show bare tit . . . well, it was colored bare tit . . . no white tit for
a couple of years and then only . . .

distraction... is that what they tell you, the trick, just distract yourself and you won't realize you have made the fatal step... no ...just take a step and am walking through the pine woods on Vitosha... though there is something a bit too forced about THAT WALK... the smell

         almost forgotten this old guy is visiting the kids out on The Island and they are talking, why doesn't he go back to Europe for a vacation... you need a vacation... you can almost smell the culture, almost taste it and he replies, the only smell he remembers from Europe is the smell of burning flesh... ain't that just another way of saying culture?   *you got to have spilt blood to go into the making of the cement... but quality blood... a reason why the highways are always falling apart in this city is*   *they mix in Italian corpses and they just don't have the same sticking*   *the same bonding qualities of Jews or Gypsies, or Irish, or*   *pick any group you like*   *there is bound to be a caucus on the corner one of these days...*

though a certain sadness... cancel   *just a moment... was having stitches out and the dentist was a woman with a ff at the end of her name*
Azim govori malko Bulgarski...
eventually after the tale
         ...there are so few Bulgarians in this country

Gosho had told Piko who was to tell him:
     Welcome, you ain't going anywhere.
Gosho smiled with the ambiguity of *it*. He was enjoying the power of the unknown. Of course nothing is unknown. Everything is worked out —or, rather, to turn ponderous in the chair—everything is known, only the details change ... are capable of being changed.

Niki confused the details with everything. He hungered after meaning in the details. Every time I turned on a smile; every time I said a kind thing about his mother . . . his brother   Niki seized on it (to give a literary aura to these thoughts), seized on it like the naturally appearing and appreciative dog kept in reserve with his bone, for such jobs . . . seized on a smile and forgot.

Give a man a detail he can get his teeth into . . . the distraction will allow you to move a razor across his throat. By the time the tastebuds have picked up the blood taste.

Piko, tell him: This is it.

How I would love to lurch out of here. To the clarity of the Arctic or Antarctic. To bathe my eyes with white snow and circle my tongue about clear icicles as when a child watching (this is one of those memories I should have, so do have though I cannot be sure if I did actually have it) the icicle melt at the edge of the roof . . . and beyond the bright sun . . . always bright in the memory . . . must be the function of memory to add light and sometimes darkness when appropriate . . . and in the yard the nerve endings of trees in winter, a subject fit for the poets.
I could go on and the palm of my hand
                        though the itch of the rope

"Let us settle about our affairs in the Balkans. Your armies are in Rumania and Bulgaria. We have interests, missions, and agents there. Don't let us get at cross-purposes in small ways. So far as Britain and Russia are concerned, how would it do for you to have ninety per cent predominance in Rumania, for us to have ninety per cent of the say in Greece, and go fifty-fifty about Yugoslavia?" While this was being translated I [Churchill] wrote out on a half-sheet of paper:

Rumania	
Russia	90%
The others	10%
Greece	
Great Britain (in accord with U.S.A.)	90%
Russia	10%
Yugoslavia	50-50%
Hungary	50-50%
Bulgaria	
Russia	75%
The others	25%

I pushed this across to Stalin, who by then had heard the translation. There was a slight pause. Then he took his blue pencil and made a large tick upon it, and passed it back to us. It was all settled in no more time than it takes to set down.

No priest on hand. I am surprised at Gosho's lack of ingenuity. I would have thought he'd have had one of those doddering old men standing in the corner mumbling something about something to something to worry about something I am supposed to have and be worrying about at this final moment . . . A certain lack of planning on his part. Or a lack of humor, maybe that is it . . . and I without a sense of humor commenting on his lack of humor.

No final memory of table top and items that had meant something . . . no last photograph in mind of shoes in a closet . . . nothing to evoke any feeling one way or the other. There will be nothing to hold on to. People like to be comforted by easy emotions. They like worn shoes, a book half-read, a pipe gone out . . . a flower pressed between the pages of a book by Yavarov.

That morning I had known. Allow me this traditional listening to the bones, to the: *I had a feeling something was going* . . . I closed down my eyes, my ears, my sense of smell . . . I did not want any easing back so as to regret some trifle. If I was going to regret, it would be the large things: not seeing the Grand Canal, not being able to walk across the Seine, not to be able to sail to America, not to walk upon the ice fields of Greenland. I am not prepared to be given a pair of worn out shoes as the last sigh, turning back . . . look over shoulders . . . get out the violins, Piko . . . surely you have been told to have the violins here for the final minutes!!!!!

Not even broken on the wheel of fate . . . no, broken, yes . . . but from getting on the train at the Gare de Lyon though when was the decision made, was any decision made . . . is all this just stale thought from too long ago . . . that was what we were talking about last season . . . or better was it back when I began saying:

I might go back

I should go back

don't you think I should go back

and a month is supplied and then a date becomes necessary because what would I say to people who ask: you . . .

Yes, I did not go because   and there came a day when I did not have anything to say, so I went, was gone . . .

Preserved the relatives from having to attend at hospital after myself

. . . keeping a family tradition, you could say: father   brother   done to death in the street, gunned down, killed, shot down . . . dead in the street with the strangers looking on appraising the pool of blood, a pool of blood just a pretty image . . . the blood on the paving blocks and them dead . . .

I know there is something in this.
I am sure there is.
Just dead.

Squabbling with the worms he'll be. They won't get his face or his hands. The party kept those bits of Gosho to put on display in his marble box. Giving them a song and dance, I'll be you . . . but such dreary music, just designed to get you in step and one two three right into . . .

They will chew me, all of me, that is left after the lye has done with it does.
Done, just done, and gone.

Past.
Today.
Future.
Everything is in the manipulation of those words. You got to keep in step with the word being invoked. Cloppered, I was, and still don't know where it was coming from. The past put my head on the block and the future was in pieces of paper I didn't see. The moment today, just didn't jump fast enough. Cornered on a street. Surrounded and I was dead.

To take flight—was that even a possibility? I am sure it'll be asked. How can it not be asked? The question puts me up against the wall. Head being bent forward.
To lie on the ground with just the spark still in the brain connected to

eye watching him walking forward, unholstering revolver, pulling back
hammer, to administer . . . a nurse late at night to calm the fever.

*No dream, no final catharsis. That is not possible. If you ask me why,
I would be at the famous loss to explain. Nikola was done to death.
Gosho . . . of him there are rumors of being taken up in an airplane
and the pressure in the cabin suddenly disappearing . . . Piko went
back to the mountains and is still there with his pear   plum   cherry
trees . . .*
*I could give him a branch over which he will swing a rope, one day.
or there will be a trolley on Dimitrov Boulevard, not able to stop in the
ice of a January in front of a movie theatre, make it the . . .* Kino
showing for the twentieth time a revival of Zorba the Greek.

N.P.
Citizen of Sofia
Bulgarian
Orthodox
Unmarried
Literate
Not convicted.

As quick to get away from this country as possible into World War II.
World War II.
Thirty million people dead and you reduce it to two stick figures, two
cartoon figures exchanging bits of paper. You got to be kidding. What
do you know? You got to be kidding.

And there is a sister somewhere . . . but since she wasn't shot down on a
street, doesn't make the easily available literary remains.
So much of any life is left out.
A good thumping cliché, THAT one is, I'll say.

Hanged by the neck until dead. It is pointed out that some very astute
thinking went into the wording. Just a hanging of a body is not enough
. . . there has to be enough of that hanging until the person is dead.

Molotov then reopened the entire "percentages" issue. He next
proposed a seventy-five-twenty-five division for Bulgaria, Hungary,
and Yugoslavia. Eden said that the new proposal was worse than
the Russian position of the previous day. Molotov then reverted to
a ninety-ten division for Bulgaria and a fifty-fifty division for
Yugoslavia. Eden replied that this offer still did not give Britain the
voice it wanted in Bulgaria. Molotov finally suggested seventy-
five-twenty-five for Hungary and sixty-forty for Yugoslavia, an
arrangement that would enable the Soviet Union to accept a
seventy-five-twenty-five division for Bulgaria. He could go no
further than that. Eden presented a counteroffer: seventy-five-
twenty-five for Hungary, eighty-twenty for Bulgaria, and fifty-fifty
for Yugoslavia. Molotov returned to his starting point. He could
agree to fifty-fifty for Yugoslavia if Bulgaria were ninety-ten. He
argued that the British should have as little interest in Bulgaria as in
Rumania, since both states were Black Sea, not Mediterranean,
countries. The Russians hoped that the British would do for the
Soviet Union in the Black Sea what the Russians were prepared to
do for Britain in the Mediterranean. Bulgaria, after all, was not
Greece, Italy, Spain, or even Yugoslavia.

Eden remained adamant. Molotov now said that he thought
Stalin might agree to seventy-five-twenty-five for Bulgaria if
Britain agreed to sixty-forty for Yugoslavia. . . .

The next day, October 11, Molotov offered a compromise
formula, which conceded to the British a 20, rather than a 10,
percent voice in Bulgaria. Overall, Molotov now proposed an
eighty-twenty division for Hungary and Bulgaria and stayed with

fifty-fifty for Yugoslavia. But what was the practical difference between 10 and 20 percent? This new division for Hungary and Bulgaria, as Molotov explained it, indicated Soviet acceptance of Eden's idea that the Allied Control Commission in Bulgaria should act on the instructions of the Soviet High Command but "with participation" of British and American representatives. After some discussion Eden said he thought that the new formulation for Article 18 on the proportioned responsibilities for the Allied Control Commission in Bulgaria would be acceptable. Molotov hoped that the same formula would be applied to Hungary.

And so matters rested. Churchill's original proposal was applied to Rumania, Greece, and Yugoslavia, but an eighty-twenty division was applied to Bulgaria and Hungary. Stalin and Molotov had extracted from Churchill and Eden a higher percentage for the Soviet Union than the seventy-five-twenty-five division for Bulgaria and the fifty-fifty division for Hungary that Churchill reported in his *Triumph and Tragedy*. The Russians had successfully blocked British and American efforts to gain substantial participation in the Bulgarian armistice.

Just dragging this out, Piko is muttering. Enough, enough. Surely you have inflicted your death on me for more minutes than is decent. And you a defender of real people and not the abstraction . . . you would think, you, of all people would have a little decency, a little real concern for this, me, this man, me, Piko, standing before you, to get it over with so I can go about my job of work and leave for the night.

There was not a moment's silence before, during or after the moment when he.
Of course there was no way of knowing and by the time people found out

to a dog a dog's death

it was already a moment from the past . . . and no one was going about organizing memorial meetings within the borders of this country.
To have the memory of one's death flung to the four corners of the earth and there gather people to remember. There must be some classical myth to express this fate.
Beyond me, I am afraid.

To choose how one is going to die is a type of ambition. Doesn't rank up there with making a million or climbing Everest or . . . blonde girls seem to come to mind . . .

What is this thing called heroism?
A cheap thrill, but I guess it's better than watching the tube.

We have, all of us, memories of stories about how men were forced to pawn their medals in hock shops so they could go forth and do combat with whatever devil he or she . . . no, only men were going forth when those stories were being told, to do combat with the bottle, a line of poetry, a woman who would or wouldn't . . . a situation.
Of course the situation.

Henry Miller: better to be a live coward than a dead hero.

After a conversation with the nephew of Nikola Petkov

His father was killed in the First Balkan War by cholera . . . more men died of cholera than were killed by bullets. I had been born in London where my father was in the diplomatic service. My mother stayed on in England and I had a nurse and I was thrown out of the country, England, as an enemy alien during the First World War, this little kid knee high... I had some schooling in England and then lycee and university in Paris like Nikola... we called Nikola, Kolya, and I was called Demy... I took my mother's name because there were no other men in the family... so as to carry on the name. Petko, Kolya's older brother, had a son with the same name as mine, Demy, but he either drowned or was boiled to death... they had a woman from the country and sometimes people from the country can be very stupid... she had put him next to this tub of boiling water and went away for a minute... when she came back the baby Demy had fallen into the tub and was either boiled or drowned... so I took or was given my mother's name so the name would not die out... but like Kolya, I, too, am a bachelor... I never married: first I was a soldier and then in the diplomatic corps... it was no life for a man with a wife and children... and you know what the communists do with the wife and children who get left behind ... in prison or worse—so it was all for good.

Petko was the older brother... he had a large library; he was very outgoing and was a good public speaker. He had that library which was given to Kolya but it was burned during the bombing of Sofia by the English and Americans... the English used incendiary bombs and the Americans high explosives... we never married and this life... he does not use the word EXILE
Kolya lived in the shadow of his brother who you know was shot down on the same day that Stambolyski was shot down only a year later in August, 1924.
The Petkov family monument is the largest one in the Sofia cemetery and when they come from the country to lay wreaths for Stambolyski they leave them at Petkov's mausoleum because no one knows where Stambolyski is buried.
But they are all dead... I know where they buried Kolya in that cemetery. I brought flowers and a little box but when I went back the next day the box and flowers had disappeared... I was shown the grave by a man who was very afraid... but I did know...
Kolya was timid   he had a woman friend in Paris and another in Sofia but that is a long time ago that is his personal life... he couldn't marry   what sort of life would that be for a woman and children   they had killed his father and they had killed his brother and often I heard him say, they will kill me too... how could you

marry knowing this?

After 1944, I guess, it was in the elections of 1945 or '46 they were looking for candidates to run for parliament and they wanted me to run with my last name and I could run in this country district   the people were anti-communist... Kolya took me aside and I was not to tell a soul... he didn't want me to run because they would then kill me, also   he wanted me to live.

In Paris we lived on the Left Bank   this is in the 1920s, 1930s Kolya didn't have to work   he was from a wealthy family   they had houses and land... he was from the high bourgeoisie... and had been in the diplomatic corps... we went to the Café Flore... there were artists and so many refugees... Bulgarian artists... he read   can't remember any particular authors   he liked La Rouchefoucauld, the Maxims and used them in his writing... his writing is very fine... his Bulgarian is very good

Literature wasn't very present in his life   there is not much literature in Bulgaria... yes, Yavarov and Vazov but Vazov tells the national story... that's why he's popular. I was a student in Sofia when Vazov died and they had all the school children march in his funeral procession... In Bulgaria you either leaned towards the west, England and France, or towards the Russians... my grandfather fought with the Bulgarian detachment at Shipka... remember it was Bulgarians, Cyril and Methodius, who invented the alphabet... now it is said everything comes from the Russians but this isn't true

Kolya was an inch or so taller than my five-foot-five or so

Downstairs to meet Petkov. I recognized him in the back of the cab ... his hand shakes a little... he is old but I recognize him as a Petkov from having seen the pictures of Kolya... yes, I have the same shape of head but the nose is different; Kolya's was very long and curved... mine is smaller... their heads are rectangular... sort of Aztec in profile...

Demy's skin is very white and his eyes are light brown...

Dimitrov, Chervenkov, Stalin enjoyed killing   there are some people who just do...

When I was escaping from Yugoslavia to Italy near Trieste we were in a little group being led by this man who I knew to be in the security forces because he was wearing a long leather coat... he was telling me he was risking his life to show us the way to the frontier... I thought then he must be joking... he knew where he was walking and he was in the security forces... later when we got to Trieste we were told that the other group of people whom we had seen waiting to cross, they were ordinary workers, Hungarians and Romanians, had all been shot down... then it dawned on me that they didn't even tell their own security forces who were to be shot down... if it was known which groups were to be shot down it would be easy to figure this out and the whole country would have left... so I then knew why this security agent had been telling me he was risking his life...

Kolya was not religious though he did take communion before he died... you must remember at the turn of the century there was this movement for separating church and state... but he was not a very religious man... this priest told me that when he was taken to be hanged he was shouting... you are murderers, you murderers ... never did he stop
I asked, why didn't they become communists: Because they believed in private property... as simple as that.

Who's to hear you scream:
                         murderer... murderer...
Their ears are already marked for elimination and my ears...
            I've heard the tune before... no hook into my flesh... as
expected as the shit to come out of your asshole.

Another corpse stuffed into the earth... though a scratch remains deep enough behind twenty-six years later, in the heat of a New York summer...
what of all the
and every day they trundle more and more corpses

What gets left behind to live
          to live
          are living.

Postcard views of Paris: Notre Dame
                    Boulevard St. Michel with an artist in beret,
moustache and a cocked eye
          Arc de Triomphe
          Eiffel Tower
          which bridge . . . of course, late night and . . . throw in
fog, a man collapsed against the wall, a broken bottle by his side.
Assassin. Assassin, he is shouting into the fog.

The mastika is not chilled, Piko is saying. No slivers of ice to dissolve
on my tongue. Wouldn't you like to have a tongue that could feel the
frozen sting of Mastika? A nodding head won't get you anywhere.

As long as you hold on to those slivers of ice, that taste of slivers of ice,
there is nothing they can do.

I am sure. Don't lecture me. It is not I who is leaving this world.

Her flesh would not allow me to forget.
Poetry.
Words, in other words, how they *do* creep in between people. If I said
her name I would have to say the other woman's name and then we are
right back to first love and the rhapsody which is entailed.
On the other hand.

I will say something, I will write something, when the moment is right.
They'll be shoveling dirt upon my face when the moment is right.

Anniversary of Death of Bulgarian Patriot
Statement by Under Secretary Smith
September 22, 1954

Seven years ago tomorrow Nikola Petkov was hanged by the Bulgarian Communist Government because he dared to oppose it. As the leader of the opposition, Petkov waged a courageous struggle for representative government, justice, and human liberties, but his voice was silenced in the traditional Communist manner. Since his death the forces against which he fought have gained full control in Bulgaria.

The Bulgarian Communist regime, by means of the judicial murder of Nikola Petkov, demonstrated once again its callous disregard for human rights and fundamental freedoms. It has continued to conduct itself in this manner, thereby not only violating the provisions of the Treaty of Peace but also the dictates of justice and humanity.

The American people and the other peoples in the free world have not forgotten Nikola Petkov. His self-sacrifice remains an inspiring example to free men everywhere. To the millions of oppressed peoples behind the Iron Curtain Petkov is justly a symbol of determination that some day they will again have governments of their own choosing.

I read myself.

Am I an open book, as some will claim after I have been dead for some time?

What more do you want to know, they will ask at the young man sitting there, his tongue wrapped around itself.

You just had to meet Niki, as you say his name; just meet Kolya as we
called him, as he was known to his intimate friends.

Yes, I do read myself, but I do not reread.
Once read a book, a piece of prose is done for me.
Is that how you should come to read this book which I have
become   there in Rio, in New York, in Paris, in Munich?
Though not a single line to hammer me firmly into the earth of
literature.

It was impossible for me to reflect. There was never the time. I had to be
here. There was always a place to be. I am not being cute. So much to
do and then I was presented with the possibility of going to a place
where my language would always be a rare occasion.

If I had . . . but there was not that word IF within my experience. From
the moment of my birth . . . well, that stretches the point . . . just
because The Old Man was killed   though once Petko was dead and
little Demy   if we Bulgarians read Greek—

Americans are such a happy race. They carry it with them and it is
painful   sometimes   to be in the same room with them. They even
take this statement as an insult. Yes, they do.
They can always go home. Home is not stuffed with as many corpses
and the stuffing has not been going on for so many years.
They are striving with all their might to fill up the earth with rotting
flesh.
They have given it, as they say, *the college try*. Cyril used that
expression.
                    We will give it the old college try
A happy race oozing optimism.

What did I know about the deal . . . what deal . . . what arrangement,
what coming to terms with the reality of power, with the presence of our
Russian friends . . .
Did I realize how wide the ocean is?
Did I realize how short the American memory is?
Did I know England was now a second-rate power with the pretensions
of an empire?
And France, did a French person ever worry about anything beyond his
own skin . . . and even that was in conflict with the demands of the stuff
inside the package.
Ignorance is . . .
I wanted to be where I was and am.

The organization would use tommy guns and not throw confetti
Is it to be struck dumb that we are given tongues in the first place and
ears that will get clogged up and eyes that will dim?
Whatever I say will be used against me. No protest will absolve
me.
They have me.
            No, it is not true I beat my mother every morning at eight
o'clock.
The skill of theirs. Yes, they have all the skills . . . or power . . . they
checked me into the corner where my mouth can only work in their
favor.
And they know this.
How I envy them!

For the longest time I thought that things would be different. That after
all we, they, were all Bulgarians. They knew what people said about us
and they had always criticized those who did those things which people
attacked us for, for which we had gotten our reputations.

Dirty Bulgarians.
Untrustworthy.
Underhanded.
Will hit you only when you are down.
Have you ever met an honest one, one whose word is his bond?
Have you . . .

To remember always: no one gives a shit what you are doing.
You will get nothing from it.
All praise will arrive too late.
Just try to remember
it's very difficult because each day has to be lived, each day has to be
greeted, out of bed, to face the mirror, to eat, to walk
Each day and that awful momentum.   But it all means nothing in the
end.
On the other hand

A center of attraction
hostile elements
defeatest activity
constructive program
uttered the slander
indiscriminate repudiation of the achievements
malicious and slanderous attacks against our friend the Soviet
Union
fallen under the influence of slanderous campaigns
hostile and slanderous descriptions
same negative attitude
denied the importance of the labor
               enthusiasm   emulation and shockwork
big plants and big chimneys which will never operate and serve as
nests for crows and owls

slanders against the Government policy
improper comparisons
slanders and threatens
appeals for disobedience

They have all the words and they control the grammar, the tenses.
They give you no place to begin. You are always trying to catch
up.
There is no answer except to run or to stay and wait for gravity to do its
neat job of work.
As it does.

Not fast enough, Piko shouts. Not fast enough.

I told myself.
I took myself down the path, not led, be sure to note that.
No one to turn to.
By myself after asking advice and having to close my ears, as the saying
goes.
Down the path and . . .

You can say that again, Piko says.

If you had known, the young man asks, would you have done anything
differently?
No.
Are you sure?
As far as I can tell there was never a moment when the end was in

doubt, I am sorry to say.

Are you sure?

I am. To say I would have done things differently is to deny, the rope, the presence of Piko, this room, this country . . . it is everything I have wanted because it happened.

That gets very mystical.

I have never been accused of that and PLEASE keep it to yourself, if you must.

Tired, so tired, eyes closing even though there is still so much to be done.

You must be kidding.

Tired. So tired. It comes as a relief to know there is an end.

The stomach is banging against the throat. To somehow forget biology. It is impossible to strangle yourself with your own bare hands.

Ain't that something? The sort of thing that stops you dead in the middle of a café conversation. To go away in awe. How some men get their reputations. A series of these conversation stoppers. While the rest of mankind is content to be sitting in a tub of slowly grown cold water, drained away to sitting there in the egg of chilled enamel. The long slow drag of a fingernail against rough slate.

So much life, yet, all this death.

Dying, Piko says, again washing out a bucket he discovered in the corner of the room. If only you hadn't looked forward so much to this day.

That is not true. Only a literary mind could say such a thing and, thank god, you, Piko, are not of that sort.

To be turned into some sort of weird child with his head under the blanket pretending though I know this is not pretending, after all I am a 55-year-old man who has been a man of power, a man of place, of a family that has always been known . . . true, a family that does not go back to the dawn of creation but back far enough so the origin of the wealth is not talked about . . . a man, get me, a man and here I am with the rope about my neck and a sidekick with a mop and bucket who knows who I am and is in a hurry to get IT OVER WITH   GET IT OVER WITH

Filled with rage   rage against
just if
just if
just if
but before that   before all of those JUST IF's there was
                              this
                              just this

So, where's the interest in this man, dangling at the end of a rope?
In the silence of the answer.
Who cares for the dead?
They are dead and are mourned by the dead. Well, they should, no one else is on duty tonight.
Petkov twists in the breeze.
There is a breeze coming from a door opened suddenly.
Don't worry, it is not a reprieve.
I have not been leading you along to grab you, finally, by the coat collar of your emotions and fling you into a discussion of what if.
He is going to be dead, soon enough.

No reprieve.
No dark comedy of a reprieve.

Kolya was not a likable person.
Isn't that refreshing?
We are going to have no delightful tales of baby heads being patted,
flowers arranged gracefully on mahogany table tops, a slice of music
running in the head even as the blood is being cut off to the brain.
The heart is set to explode.
Inquiries have to be made as to whether he ever sat in The
Bambouk.
He will be set into The Bambouk. Complaints will be heard from the
nitpickers saying, I have got the times all screwed up, stage sets
miscued.
The National Theatre is just across the street. That is justification
enough.
Or think of this as a poem. Just because The Bambouk possibly was not
there . . . back then . . . we can imagine, can we not?

Of course it is not, of course it is not so unusual in this century of the
innocent dead. And there is always the chance they will have to
rehabilitate Petkov. They will have to find a street to give his name to
. . . they will name a factory after him. There might even be a
stamp.
I am being naive. Petkov was not a communist. Only communists are
rehabilitated by communists. A little slip-up in the history writing.

My man Petkov ain't no ticket to the Black Sea for further research.

To be far away. I never wanted to be far away, unlike so many people. I
could have traveled. There was nothing to stop me.
I could have sailed to New York. I could have gone to China, to Japan,
to Australia, to South Africa, to Peru.
I could have.
I did not.
I do not remember if I dreamed.

There is no articulation possible against the rope cutting into the skin.
By the time   by that time   and it is always that time   now   anymore   forever more   the rope is always there with an undreaming
personality.

We must grow fond of the rope. It is our reminder. It is my end. It is the
instrument of my end. The doing of the deed of history.

The famous nightmare of the Irishman. I will not awake. I will not be
suffering from a stiff back joint in the hips gone bad, a muscle in the neck
pulled.

Was reminded, one of the cruelist blows: **you are not married.**
                                        have no family of your
own.
And the man is asking me about **78 kilograms of washing soap** . . . and
I am telling him my sister is living in the house and your man is saying I
need the soap to wash my conscience and I tell him his wit is useless to
me.
We keep the soap in the house to wash out mouths after the words I
hear. How common all these people have become.
Trying to tell a joke and I am supposed to listen to it. You got to have
soap.

No wife, to wait, to mourn, to write THAT letter, to forget and put the best face on the what has come to pass. No one to wait who has been within a sentence.

Something always a little disappointing. You would think . . .
Is this the sort of language . . .
Come on. I must be kidding myself or yourself or . . .
A long way from whether to bury the corpse and the tragedy that rolls on . . .
to fuck one's father, mother, son, brother
how   to   what was he going on about: was I in favor of the campaign to collect fodder?
Now, was I?
And the whole nation went to sleep every night wondering: was enough fodder collected during the day . . . maybe we should schedule night-time fodder collection campaigns.
I shook my head right into the prepared loop of rope.
That's what they'll say.

I must now show disappointment. Everything is as it is supposed to be. That is the glory of everything that has happened.
I must remember to tell them sitting in The Bambouk: everything is as it is supposed to be.
Would that be labeled negative criticism . . .
I'll have another slice of cake and a bottle of orange soda. It is too early for a little glass of Mastika.

Piko's ears burn with the thought of Mastika.
Come again . . . shouldn't it be, his throat is thirsty for . . . surely I am entitled to a little sensory displacement.

Petko had heaped up books and went and was shot down. I was expected to root among the books for a reason, was I, for his death, for his being picked out . . . no, I was expected to find consolation.

The American bombs took all the books away.
Cleared the air of the rooms through which I walked.
I was not confused about why I was doing things.
I just did them.
I was to be killed.
I was to die
Did I need to know anything more.
Ah, Petko . . . none of this lingering around for you.
Every word was on the tip of your tongue. The words did not congregate in the back of your throat like men escaping the church service in the halls of the church.
Ah, Petko . . . that fool compares us

I so stink of myself. My nose rebels, my eye rebels, my tongue rebels and my life is leaving me.
This long drawn out . . .
and they used to snicker at the Shakespeare death scenes . . . to see how long the dying could be prolonged.
We are not Chinese, one reviewer wrote. We do not take delight in seeing how long the life takes to be extracted.
We know the intestines are X number of feet . . . this is being taken down in the United States . . . the metrics are translated in time . . . we know how long the intestines . . . we do not need to see every inch to know that the person, the character, is going to the final roundup.

Give them an inch and they'll take a mile every time.

Hoisted up, not even a step into . . . was it supposed to be eternity I was stepping into . . . was that the poetic escape from this shit leaking down the inside the leg . . .

Nag. Nag. Nag.
Using the name of Petko. What am I supposed to do? I come after him. I
cannot reverse the order of our births. If only I had come before . . .
both of us might still be alive.
But how would we be alive?
If
His corpse is heavy upon my shoulders. But not heavy enough to break
this rope.

Unlikely I am to be the hero. But isn't that always the case? Who comes
out of the womb with the newspapers setting his name into headlines,
the scholars to their task of sorting out the rights and the wrongs.

As I have   before   if only I had been Greek. Fate would explain
it all. Shrug of shoulders and . . . into the . . . will I be accused of
wanting the Greek church back amongst us with their oppressive liturgy
and the kids being beaten for speaking Bulgarian in class? Gemeto
would go on about that for hours. I was not much for listening to his
tales of woe; does the countryside produce any other sort of tale?

Please do not think badly of the rope,
                of this man, Piko,
                of this room
                of this stool
                of this year, of this hour, of these minutes . . .

How could one waste one's time
just to be worn down

yet not to give in—
and for no particular reason,
ain't that the kick in the head

If those peasants, forgive me, had dared to ask: Kolya, why did you do
or not do what you have or have not done . . . instead of all this beating
around the bush . . .

It's the mockery of the form that bothers. A trial is always bad theater.
It is the staging of a Mass. Though there are two possible conclusions,
unlike the Mass which has only one.
I am teasing . . . twisting at the end of my rope.
NOW I AM DOING THAT, am I not?

God, swords, and language that battled it out with the clouds.

It was proved: I had two entrances to my house. Isn't that nice to
know?
Something to hold on to.
Here I have only an entrance to make, have made an entrance and I will
not be here to make my exit.
Piko and I have both used the same door.

An intimate friend visits by means of the back door. That sent a chuckle
through the crowd.
Throw them another bone.
Not that I am suggesting they are seeking a bone to gnaw upon.
We all know what is being said.
We are all men in this room, right, Piko . . . or do I have to talk about
what happens across the border in Greece: that famous Greek . . .
Piko blushes.

With all the books heaped up I felt no need to read. It was enough to read the faces of the people that passed, as we sat at the café tables. Whole epics walked by and were forgotten: where is the poet of what is seen from café tables? We have a legion singing the praises of the natural order of things: the birds, the mules, the camels, the maple trees, the linden trees, the pine, the stones . . . legions of them, and not a single one of them will admit to getting wet when they put their foot into that beautiful nature of theirs.

When was the last time you heard of a glass of Mastika growing from a tree: answer me that.

There is no answer to any of it. No cleverness was going to get in the way of my being in this room.

To live in a country with a tiny literary tradition. Can it be imagined: a French prosecutor reading *Gone With the Wind* and then in an open courtroom to quote from it . . . and our prosecutor is saying Marko is like that woman in the novel . . . now if he had said in the film, in the film he would have had everyone . . .

cancel all of this . . .

a lurch into literary taste.

How in this place, this place far from Paris, far from London . . . far even from Moscow and Berlin   no, cancel Berlin . . . I don't want to have fascist thoughts . . . to think of Berlin is to have a fascist thought, I am sure the man would say . . . Marko, would Rhett Butler turn on his heel and walk away from you?

He reminds us of the hero of Margaret Mitchell's novel and I was in touch with a woman who translated: *A Moment in Peking, A Night in Bombay.*

What will they, who come after us, think we were doing?

Petko burned the only bridge I had to life. Not exactly. His death tore

down the only bridge I had away from this place. I had to come back.
All the other roads were blocked with his death. I did not want to end up
in New York living in rooms, afraid to walk on the streets late at night,
afraid to be found dead in the hallway . . . to have to live in tiny rooms
with picture frames on the wall, nothing in the picture frames . . . all my
photographs lost, all my relatives living on only as names . . . and me
just living on waiting to die, sitting with cane between legs on a sagging
plastic milk carton, looking at the world, jealous of all those who will
outlive me, who will find more, who will have done more, who . . .

Ah, Piko, you are keeping me from a fate worse than this death. I will
not have to lust after snazzy color photographs.

Tired of hearing the kids playing cowboys and red Indians . . . decided
to invent the new game of fascists and partisans
how long will it last
a certain cycle. Must give them credit for at least attempting to invent a
new kids' game . . . eventually the debunking will come along
the underground will be treated as a joke . . .
In that I might as well talk about the wood beam overhead suffering pain
from the pull of the rope about it, about my neck . . .
As confused as you can get and then leave it all alone. I had my part and
did my part.

Full silence.
I should lean across the table and tell you about my time in the
camps.
Not in one of those camps.
Just a camp.
There have been so many camps since the British invented them during
the Boer War.

I was privileged because they knew who I was. They knew my name.
Here I am also known.
I am known, too well known.
But at least I will still be known in twenty years.
How awful.
Here they are not afraid of me. I can tell them there will be hell to pay if anything happens and I will be rewarded by a choir of laughter.
Laughter is so rare in prison.
In the camp, the guards observed the law.

Eighth Anniversary of Death of Bulgarian Patriot
Statement by Under Secretary Hoover

September 22, 1955

Eight years ago tomorrow Nikola Petkov, a great Bulgarian patriot, was hanged in Bulgaria. After a trial which made a mockery of justice, he was judicially murdered on September 23, 1947, in order that communism in his country might triumph.

Nikola Petkov was a courageous liberal and a valiant defender of democracy in his country. His countrymen will never forget the boldness and selflessness with which he and his colleagues fought Communist injustice even after their cause seemed lost. That the Communist press in Bulgaria should finally have described his death as an "imperative state necessity" is striking evidence of the vigor of his struggle.

Although Nikola Petkov's voice and pen have been silenced, his spirit still lives. His devotion to the cause of justice and democracy will ever serve as inspiration to his countrymen and to all liberty-loving people who look forward to the day when the captive peoples can once again live in freedom under governments of their own choosing.

I was envied when I was a kid. They all wanted an older brother to look after them, to be able to say, if you do *that* my brother will . . . or . . . did you see what my brother did . . . did you . . . aren't you jealous of my good fortune.
Eaten by those words, those memories. Now.

To tell the truth. And if the truth does not agree with the truth they have decided I should be telling, as the truth . . .
There is the smell of word splitting, of philosophy, of the cafés . . .
Must all the talk of cafés end in a puddle of urine on the floor?
I would tell you anything you wanted to hear. You are deaf to my words.
You do not understand my language.

My rooms are very important.
This room is very important.
A room in the prison built by my father.
At least I can say my rooms were not in the house of my father. My life was in the house of my father and he is six feet under the earth, bullet holes to keep him company.
A certain crudeness. Yes?
A bedroom, a dining room which may or may not be shared with the sister and brother-in-law upstairs, a hall to pace, two drawing rooms.

An addict of nothing stronger than newspapers . . . or is that the final addiction? Unlike heroin which rots only ambition or alcohol which destroys the liver and some of the brain . . . well, most of the brain eventually—newspapers remove the heart and the brain . . . the eye no longer sees . . . clogged with words, with pictures . . . with facts piled upon facts and ... comes home rather late, either from the newspaper office or he may have been with ... well, he is a bachelor ...

To lie down with one's futility ... nothing can come of this ...

Nature is in its right place in this city of Sofia: there at Vitosha. A city is only a city if it is near the mountains. A city must have a mountain. Well, a certain kind of city. Paris and London are cities without a mountain. Both have heaped up hills of corpses at distant places.

Vitosha. How many poems. Even Americans have written poems about tramping through woods on Vitosha, in the snow. The French have been here

VITOSHA

Orange splashed in a distant sky
never overhead
never marking these steps
always out there.

To the left, tracks,
recent animals—
underneath packed snow
dirty from walkers.

And then naturally the dark
fear comes from the unknown, says the pedant
I say, it comes from waiting
for what has happened
to happen again.

If only I was the true spirit of negation. My career would have been set in Paris. I would have been launched into those dusty rooms, sitting behind a mahogany desk, the top covered with leather, writing of possibility: a group of villagers has been massacred and their bodies stuffed down the village well; of one still alive, halfway down into the well, there midst the past . . . what thoughts to imagine in his head . . . how to prepare during the day to dream at night what it was like: to become his thought, yes, a man, not a woman because it would be too easy to impose thought upon a woman, a woman not yet able to claim her own self from the keeping of man to imagine the waiting . . . and the waiting.

And the lawyer has to go after poor Koev. How else can I describe him? Do not think me full of pity. I will not undertake the arrogance, the awfulness of pity, an exercise in feeling, in proving we see the blind woman begging for the funeral of the dead baby in her arms. Better to have cultivated the supposition that the baby is not dead, only drugged, or the baby is not hers but borrowed, already dead and preserved, as a way to embarrass people into giving; people for whom death is something to be put far, far from the mind, to appear only on posters either with a star or a cross or blank above the head and the dates of the completion of one's   if I said sentence . . .
what happened to Koev
nothing unusual   beaten into saying what was expected of him

Should I make a litany of the names, remembering the expression on the French face when I replied:
                    I am Bulgarian
I could have been saying: I come from the moon . . . though the moon is closer to most people in France than Bulgaria . . . this is back then . . . now every French person knows about that Bulgarian export: Sylvie Vartan . . . and some know Tsvetan Todorov or Julia Kristeva . . .
So, I make a list in no particular order:

Stamboliski
Dimitrov
Vazov
Yavarov
Gichev
Boris
Ferdinand
Stambolov
Levski
Botev
Father Paisi

An epidemic of handshaking has broken out all over the country.
Wherever you look you see two hands shaking . . . some are pink, some
are red, some are green . . . some are black . . . some are spat upon if a
man has a good spit. Only I am seeing these hands.
I too participated for the longest time in the disease of shaking hands.
I tried, after, to come to some understanding but my hand would not be
there attached to an arm reaching out . . . I could no longer
　　　　　　　　　my neck was eyed and

Exhaustion, the complement of the writing being done at one in the
morning, windows open to the avenue noise, a mad woman screaming
at the stars which are pieces of broken glass hammering at the top of
her skull, drunks breaking bottles, the screech of a car . . . and his
exhausted body giving in to the force of gravity.

Have to turn away, once in a while, just for a moment.

A luxury not permitted by himself.

I do turn away.

Of course my hand shakes, my arm shakes, my whole body shakes because there are no words in my mouth to answer. Can you not read the flesh of my flesh and remember when it was like this for yourself: as a child and being afraid to walk home from school because they are there waiting . . . is that too homey for you . . . you who accuse me of lying in the very flesh of my body, shaking is to be interpreted as a lie: you have been seeing too many melodramas at the cinema.

If I was truly crushed do you not think I would lie on my bed and chew chew the life out of my wrists?

I am caught in a vacuum created by your accusation . . .

Elemental scientific explanations carry no water for you.

Of course I am an invention. What else could I be? I keep myself in existence. I breathe, I walk, I talk, I . . . eat . . . I shit . . . I . . . and the rest: well, everybody does something like this. I have walked into a novel as I have put my head into a noose, had my head put through a noose and the rope tightened and . . . am in danger of falling into the lie of a grand metaphor.
I am here.
Yes, I am here.
I, Nikola Petkov, was alive, am alive.
Well, yes but.
The famous *yes, but*

The librarians have done me, you, an injustice. Notice how they have classified this writing.

Gemeto knew what to do. I do not envy him having to drag out his life in the constant explanation it will have to be.

Maybe he will enjoy it.

I do not think I would like living in a suburb of Washington, D.C.

Some people can live anywhere.

I would have gone to Paris.

He was said to have taken up the Protestant revenge, tennis, complete with suntan. He must have picked up these English habits in Egypt.

I replaced him and he lived on.

And lived on.

Nothing has been shown in these words. No scene has been set. No one has made an entrance or cooked a meal or taken leave of the gathering. Small talk has not been exchanged, that delaying action before the hook of a final chapter sentence propelling the reader into the next chapter.

I cannot breathe.

Her hair curved about her narrow face. She was wearing a blue sweater and began to walk away from me. We had talked and her eyes did not fear to look at me. She had to look down at me. I wanted to hold her face in the palms of my hands.

I wanted.

I wanted.

My tongue curls back and to think . . . no more than just to think . . . yes, my arm shakes, my whole body shakes to think . . . again that word . . . *to think*—just to know she will go on living and you, Piko, will be able to see her . . . though you will probably be blind to her, to the memory of blue sweaters . . .

I see only shadows of what might have been. They can only remain as shadows. I have no memory of seeing anyone I loved grow into old age. Everything is always cut short.

Cut off.
Lopped off.
And she walked away.
What else could she do?
I would have done the same.
I was once a figure of promise. No one ever looked too closely at what was being promised.
No shoes. Like a general dying in bed.

I am trying to remember what the weather during the trial was like. There was heat. People were sweating. I was indifferent to the heat, to the smells. I should not have been. If I could tell you the temperature, the presence or absence of cloud . . . would that give more substance to these words? At least, then, you would know I have lived in the physical world. That I have been aware of what goes on beyond the frontiers of my own brain box.
In this room, I am within the room of my neck and what is being done to me. There is no climate to this room. There is no weather. I hear the waves of water banging against the sides of the buckets when Piko moves them. I have   now   run out of ways to describe the room. If I told you of the light bulb as a parody of the sun . . . or should I make that
     of the moon

Nikola Petkov is 55 years old. He will not get to be 56.

I who write out this text, this novel, this prose, these words am 38 and I will be 39 as these pages are written out for the first time. Petko, the older brother who was shot down on the street in Sofia, was two years older. He would have been 57 during this trial. If he had been alive Nikola would have been in Paris.

> The author will be *42* years old when the words are turned into printing.

Fallacy of the **what if,** *the* **but** *in history. Anything to avoid having to deal with that piece of rope wrapped around the human neck, and the breath leaving the body . . . the brain might be dead by now . . . would have to lurch to the East to come up with some justification for where these words are coming from.*

At one time if I had said that a man's age was 55, I would have thought he was an old man. Now I just think of him as older than I am. We are both aware of the fact of our dying. We have both seen friends die . . . we both when we hear of someone we have known as dying or being very sick . . . wonder when it will happen to us . . .
death becomes our permanent interlocutor.

To make one's farewells to the earth, to the nation, to the city, to the people of one's birth, to the street, to the house . . . how many more before this litany drives a person to . . .
To say farewell.
To say goodbye.
To say . . .
A sunny day at the train station. The camera is aimed, the picture does not turn out . . . too much exposure, not in focus: isn't that always the way it is?
A farewell should be botched, almost.
To be on the train
Or to be on that station platform. Both have their partisans. I prefer the station platform. To travel by imagination and to not actually go.
Have I kept the leave-taking simple enough?

Had no choice in the matter.
Am almost gone away.

There is nobody left.
There is no one person left.
Well, my sister . . . yes, there is my sister. I will not deny her or her son
or her husband.
But seriously . . . have I been anything but serious—part of the problem
so far, if you ask me, Piko says. Cleaning another bucket. I hope you
have counted out the number of buckets I am meant to be cleaning.
Not even my face remains for me. There is no mirror in this room, not
even a pornographic mirror nailed to the ceiling.
I am sure they are filming my performance, getting ready for the grand
request premiere for Gosho . . . he is in good company. How else to
explain the absence of piano wire, and meat hooks?

You can't touch a human thought!
How's that for banality!
The heat of tears. The coldness of hatred. The . . .
And language covers up this thought . . . this thing you can't touch, see
I got my head in the loop and they decide to turn to linguistics to save
me. Down the hatch, you might say. I knew all along. I had studied the
law. It is a comfortable place. Anything can be proven, anything at
all.
I will not argue.
I will only . . . yes, quote Shakespeare:
             "I can not heave my heart into mouth"
That's what they should have said.
Or I should have been told . . .

A responsible man does not have time for poetry. A lyric would not

ease the rope from my neck.
It might have prevented me from . . .
I cannot allow myself this thought . . . this intangible thing . . .

I have heaped up a hill of sentiments and have been spending the
minutes flinging them into a sack to carry into . . . to carry upon my
back for all . . . or I should have attached them to my ankles to provide
more weight . . . might have done me quicker.
But no one will believe such sentiments. They will want to see the
proverbial warts. I should be seen strangling a cat. That will cut to the
bone. Maybe I was doing that as a young man. Will provide a clue to
later resignation. Final paying out of one's penance for the torturing of
cats. Remember how we tied a noose about the neck of that cat and
suspended it from a lamp post, a street or so away from the king's
palace. All night the cat would have gone on . . . No, the cat was dead
by the time we got the rope over the cross beam of the lamp post.
Somewhere mercy was discovered in the hearts of young men.

Have me compared to Hitler.
                    A Bulgarian Hitler
My politics are said to be similar to Hitler's.
That's what comes from being in a position of having cronies . . . where
did they dig up that word. It has an American air about it.
                    A Bulgarian Hitler
I have painted neither landscapes nor houses. I have not been to war. I
have not stood in front of a king's palace cheering at the announcement
of war.
I have not wished harm upon the Jewish people.
Maybe it was my trip to Moscow. To shake hands with Stalin. Were
they harking back to Hitler and Stalin's breakfast chats . . . well, at
least their men got together and ate breakfast. Found they had more in

common.

All powerful people have more in common with each other than any
simple person has with a man in power . . . with a person in power . . .
In power you get used to having yourself anticipated. Life takes on the
quality of ritual   almost the splash of Baptismal water is heard

   just Piko with his buckets, and his complaint: surely, I should be
doing something more than just moving buckets around.

TWO BULGARIANS

V is around the author's age and the son of a man who studied to be
a priest. He is a lawyer and in addition to his profession he tries to
work at psychiatry. But this is really impossible. A private life is
nearly a foreign idea, an impossible idea in Bulgaria both for
historical and current political reasons. V does not like to leave
Sofia even for a day trip to the mountains and has no desire for
foreign travel. He would travel if it were possible but without the
illusions which propel many Bulgarians into longing for going
abroad. His life is in Sofia, in his studies of human behavior and of
how people live day to day: the strangeness, the constant effort to
see all human behavior as strange . . . and thus remarkable . . . he is
interested in religion, in the translations of difficult American
novels and he celebrates with a small circle of friends the Fourth of
July because of what that holiday originally meant in 1776. He
thought for a moment before answering what he thought Nikola
Petkov had been doing: "Maybe he was showing character."

G is a difficult character to describe. Men of power are always
difficult to describe because we would like to treat them either with
irony or scorn and thus dismiss them. G is a powerful official in the
government. He travels constantly for the government: New York,
Paris, London, Ankara. We met for dinner under the lime trees and
he arrived at the outdoor restaurant on a French bicycle which he
had just brought back from Paris but this was the first time he had
the time to use it. He traveled so much he didn't have an apartment in Sofia and still used his mother's apartment as his address.
Anyone could hunger and sweat to buy an automobile but G

enjoyed his bicycle and knew what it meant to the people who saw him go by. He helped people out of an interest in helping people. He enjoyed using his power because it made him conscious of his power. He knew the limits of that power and did not seek prominence with that power. He was, as far as that is possible, a man probably content with his life. When asked about Nikola Petkov G replied, "He was just stupid."

I am said to be a patriot, a lover of the Bulgarian people, to have affection for the nation called *Bulgaria* . . . the mountains, the seacoast, the rivers
but what a dry fuck it all is . . .
the heresy hunters will jump upon my back, their pouncing will knock me down but when they rear back: nothing . . . how do you criticize dust?
Strips of flesh will be pulled from my back, if only they could: lay them drying in the sun of their poorly printed magazines and newspapers that issue from towns barely on the map.
The dead do not have the ability to argue with the living guardians of their memory.
The closer they get to my legacy, the quicker they will drive themselves into the earth.
You can hear the young people in the driveways saying they do not understand the old people sitting in the kitchen arguing in THAT language . . . it must be the wine . . . it goes to the old man's head . . . when will he be dead, finally?
How much longer will they drag this out? How can I have any friend over to the house with these relics sitting in the kitchen, arguing in that harsh language, made even harsher by futility?

And found guilty of spreading silly jokes . . . accused of spreading silly jokes . . . now there they have the possibility of a charge. One can

answer, down to the footnotes of the footnotes the accusations of being
an American agent
a British agent
a Greek agent
an agent of reaction
the corpse of Hitler
but how to answer for a joke . . . now a silly joke if it is well told . . . but I
cannot stuff the corn down the throat of this goose so words of paté
will come forth . . .

plotting a coup is easy enough to refute . . . but
I can expect to be confronted by clown makeup, maybe an exploding
cigar—

"ISMS"

SOCIALISM:	If you have two cows, you give your neighbor one.
COMMUNISM:	If you have two cows, you give them to the government and the government gives you some milk.
FASCISM:	If you have two cows, you keep the cows and give the milk to the government and the government then sells you some of the milk.
NEW DEALISM:	If you have two cows, you shoot one and milk the other and pour the milk down the drain.
NAZISM:	If you have two cows, the government shoots you and keeps the cows.
CAPITALISM:	If you have two cows, you sell one and buy a bull.

Yanked out of context . . . held up by the ears, you could say, or wouldn't: you are no president's dog.

By the neck, we have you and that's the end of it.

Could just as easily find myself

yourself, Piko, dropped back into some context or other, find yourself having to deal with a room filled with weeping, a man pacing the floor in the hall, waiting for the word . . .

No, they were supposed to have slept through this night and only found out about

from the morning papers which crowed, crowed, did they crow out my death? A new day was dawning. A new future would now be coming rolling down the pike, now that their Bulgarian Hitler was no more . . .

Let all such traitors be so warned.

Symptoms of disintegration. That's what it was called. Me: a mere symptom. And sometimes a disease to be treated with the radical cure of contempt.

This room at one time had been painted a light shade of blue. The whole room. A leftover from the time of my father . . . there must have been something in one of the advanced books he had read about the ability of color to soothe the human beast . . . the shade of light blue reduces tension and words are able to be used instead of the billy club. He might have believed this, or at least read it.

My father and you will hear me call out, MY MOTHER, just to avoid disappointing any fans of cinematic death. A mother is designed to be called upon at the moment of death. As well she as anyone.

Jean had taught French at The American School and Sergei was Russian just living in Sofia. I never asked him why . . . sometimes it is best not to ask . . . I should have . . . we would sit in The Bambouk and Sergei was talking about being cursed by his age . . . he was maybe now forty-five or so and all the women he slept with were . . . their mouths looked like a British bomb had landed . . . and their flesh . . . I could feel the fingerprints of all the previous temporary tenants . . . Oh, to be young again. Jean nodded his head: to be young again and to be led by the nose . . . by every glance, profile of breast, corner of smile and you Nikola?

I never knew what to say. I listened and went away from these conversations feeling something must be missing . . . Sergei and Jean had been young, they were no longer young, and now they were getting older. I never went through these stages: I knew everything . . . don't get me wrong . . . not know everything in the sense you might think . . . but know it is all such a short period of time . . . the span so short that to divide it at all is to use up some of that time . . .

have candles suddenly appear and tables that move be placed between us . . . the mysteries of the Orient are revealed for the first time . . .

Sergei is saying: it is the grey hair between the legs . . . Jean nods his head: the grey hair on your head between the legs of the dust grottos . . .

Yes, I have lived in the past.

That would be the poetic way to say it.

Or   the past has lived on in me: foxes wrapped in my cloak . . . or something like that . . . I claim no Spartan blood

Two corpses in my blood   and blood on my hands   whole shelves of eggs ready for the hammer, ready for the omelet.

I have not though tried to inflict the past upon anybody as some would the future.

Sergei allows the memory of young girls to fill up his fingers. He is alone because of that.

I am not being smug . . . how to convince anyone of that . . .

I walk into a room. I am seen for   for what . . . seen as this man who is *Nikola Petkov*.   I might as well be dead.

I am always being seen. I am known . . . I am a creature of the newspapers, of the history books . . . I no longer have a speck of freedom.

You will be dead

don't worry   don't worry   it is coming very soon   now

"One should listen to the useless" is a saying repeated many times in Russia
No one listens. To the saying.
How could they? They know what they are. What each of us is. It is not a pleasant situation.
To say the least.
I would not listen.
I thought I was of some use.
I was of some use.
That was . . . and there comes an end.
I did not see this.
We must listen to the voices that seem useless.
That is the exact saying.
I never did so.

A sort of final build up to the final moment. There might still be the chance to pull it off.
But no. NO NO NO NO NO NO NO NO NO NO NO NO NO NO
I was quite happy in Paris   or at least the question of happiness or the lack of happiness did not come up. I lived without a single thought as to what was going to happen to me. It is was all so much . . .
I am dead but go on squirming. The body calls out against the sentence. The mind long ago . . . but the cells, the very cells themselves, scream out to live   and I am caught in the middle of some awful film, movie . . .
I walked through the rooms late at night. Sleep was for another time.

There would be plenty of time for sleep. Nothing held my eye. I want to talk to someone . . . no, I didn't want to talk with anyone. I yawn and find my hand in front of my mouth; it is three in the morning, alone, and yet I still place my hand in front of mouth when I yawn. I am well trained.

Gosho is saying: you can write out what we want in your own words or we will write it out in our words, for you, fix your name to our words and there is nothing   don't think there is anything you can do . . . the pen is in our hand   it is filled with our words and your name is affixed to them   you can if you want supply your own words   at least do that favor to yourself
It will little matter: the confession will be published and even if there are doubts expressed, claims that it is a forgery, there are always plenty of people who will believe our side, who will say they don't know all the facts, that you can never be sure, that . . .

Not until the final moment. That is the human condition. Always hoping.
Even with the last letter written. Always time for a couple of more after the final letter. Or at least I think so   being so far away. Or so close I cannot see it being however sighted it is that prevents one from seeing what is exactly under one's nose.

I am writing to you again briefly but to the point. Some of us are falling but many more are coming to take our places . . . The tempest is approaching, but we will carry on to the end as we have pledged. The enemy has no intention of coming to its senses, of changing its policies. You were right—its program is to plunge deeper and deeper into crimes and outrages. . . .

The enemy, as you will know, is not only cruel but treacherous. However, not only the enemy but the entire world will realize what the Bulgarian people, and in particular, the Bulgarian peasant can do! . . . Even if we betray our cause, *he* will never betray it—you know him best of all.

to the committee.

I am writing to you mainly to inform you that our freedom to work is coming to an end. I heard from a reliable source that our organization will be dissolved, but the enemy will succeed no more than the fascists did . . . In any case, our work is about finished. We did what we could. Let's hope that those who can do more will . . . although at some later time . . . For you, the time of action is once more at hand. And the people's eyes turn instinctively towards you. They gnash their teeth and say: "We have launched the struggle and we will bring it to a successful end." You know our people; they never lose hope, and today they are more optimistic than ever. Their faith never fails them . . . Do not listen to any rumors. He who is not engaging in any activity never makes mistakes. Nothing has been changed and nothing will change. On the contrary we are strengthening our positions more and more. I have arranged everything the way we decided from the very beginning, maybe even better. . . .

It doesn't seem likely that we will see each other again. But if we do we will have a lot to talk over. If we don't, others in particular the People will relate these things. At least the people will survive. You are absolutely right about the people. You should also be proud of your friends. . . .

Our faith is unlimited and I know that it will be justified. Keep on working and remember that your sacrifices and work are not in vain.

Keep safe and healthy
I send you love on behalf of all of us
Yours, Nikola Petkov

Hammered with details. Eventually the brain goes numb. You are prepared to believe the first yokel who comes along sure of what he is saying as long as it's on the order of: it's going to rain; a cold night we had; a warm afternoon is just around the corner . . . something about:

3,000 Swiss cartridges

. . . didn't they realize they were echoing the Irishman's play, *Arms and the Man* . . . there is was hotels.

We could have talked about the bathing habits and got us much maligned.

Anniversary of Death of Nikola Petkov

September 22, 1956

The execution of the Bulgarian patriot Nikola Petkov on September 23, 1947, by Bulgarian Communist authorities violated all principles of justice and humanity. He was falsely charged and condemned, and the democratic Agrarian Party, which he led, was arbitrarily suppressed. On this 9th anniversary of Petkov's tragic death the Communist regime of Bulgaria remains stigmatized by these acts which it has as yet made no effort to rectify.

Nikola Petkov was one of four Bulgarian leaders who signed the armistice in 1944 which took his country out of the war as an ally of Nazi Germany. He played an active role in establishing a democratic coalition government. However, when it became evident in July 1945 that the Communist minority had usurped the powers of government, Petkov and the majority of his Agrarian followers withdrew in protest. From then until his arrest in 1947, Petkov, as the acknowledged leader of the democratic forces in Bulgaria, opposed communism in his country with unyielding courage.

By his devotion to the cause of freedom and his valiant efforts in defense of democratic principles, Nikola Petkov earned the lasting admiration and respect of the free world. The memory of his name is no less enduring than the ideals for which he struggled.

There was no money for Piko to do his traditional job. Possibly he would not have known what his traditional job was. New to the job, not yet a cynical professional, living in a world where traditions are formed into song. He just has to stand back and get among his buckets.

What are you going on about, Piko looks up.

You don't know, now do you . . . saying it in such a way to annoy . . . I shouldn't be doing this . . . however . . . an educational experience.

Piko is all ears, as the saying goes.

You were supposed to add your weight to mine and drag my body into death. As it is I linger, I struggle, my body struggles and you don't receive the extra payment from song and tradition.

I am a new man. Don't you read the paper or listen to the radio . . . This is the new Bulgaria.

It is that, I say to him. Your pocket is as empty as mine.

I would not line it with foreign gold as you did your own.

Show me this gold. Show me this gold.

They said you had it socked away.

I never had any such thing.

So you couldn't participate in the tradition even if you wanted to.

Scumbunnies, shiteaters, turnip fuckers, goat molesters, eaters of Turkish manure   to think they will each get up this morning and another day will dawn for them . . . to think . . . not for long to think. Sea treasures in the cabinet next to the bed, foreign cigarette packages, a coin from the United States, a photograph card of Clark Gable . . . no longer will the eye rest on the palm tree lamp made from shiny green cloth . . . to no longer see, to hear the old woman filling up the stove in the kitchen, the slight low thud of wooden spoon against the side of the pan . . .

Ah, Piko, they will need a razor to open your eyes after this night's drinking. I do not envy you that, but the couple of hours of later beyond even a wish.

There will be a misprint in the transcript of the trial:
>   Did these people invent these facts; did they purposely want to
>   wind the rape around their necks?

No comfort. No settlement. No allowance for irony. No humor. No
getting on a horse and riding into the sunset. No cavalry arriving in the
nick of time. The rope is not severed by an arrow, by a silver bullet, by
the slice of a saber.

Everything is as it should be, given the circumstances. Everything is
happening as it should happen.

Just another day in the . . .

Night please. Just another night in the year 1947, in Sofia . . .

Even that knowledge does no good.

Caviar was laid out on the gold plates and champagne in crystal glasses
from before the war, before the First World War . . . rimmed with gold
and delicate tracings of red in the bowl of the glass . . . harking back to
their betters, letting us know no criticism was possible and none of that
Russian champagne . . . French . . . as good as any I tasted in Paris.
Gosho knew how to lay a table and hold us in the palm of the hand . . .
many a palm has waited for me . . . there must be some sort of joke to
deal with what sits in the palm of your hand, maybe in hands and
clapping with joy, destruction . . . much too pointed and melodramatic:
got to hit them over the head or they don't get the joke.

We are a rude people. Once we have walked on a city street. Feeding
material to the journalists who have instructions to avoid complexity,
avoid, avoid, avoid.

Silence was to become the fashion in Paris. I was there silent during the
time of all the great talkers and was told that years before was the *real*
time of the true talkers . . . it is probably always so . . . we cannot

escape the sentence of our birth. We have to make do. Gosho was a talker. He liked the sound of his own voice. His many voices. Petko likes the sound of his own voice. He enjoys his voice. The look that came into a person's face when he spoke. I do not like to look at people when I speak. I see the abyss between the thought, the word, the ear . . . all that technical round about way of saying . . . the lie creeps in when we are in the midst of speaking . . . I do not like to dance my words across the eyes of a listener.

Why we lie in the dark in bed with our love, eyes closed . . . talking against the sound of the heart's beating, drumming us into a war . . .

Your Irishman Shaw knew us, knew us as a people even if he didn't like us for his own reasons . . . a certain resemblance to his own people, to his own country from what I have seen of them in Paris and being struck with the knowledge of what the English lord said of Ireland: just because one is born in a stable doesn't mean one is a donkey . . . or it could have been a mule or a horse or what have you . . . forgetting that the Christ child was born in a stable . . . of course an Englishman would forget something like that or an Irishman trying to imitate an Englishman; at least Turgenev had his Bulgarian die in Venice and be a rebel so that Levski and Botev could come after . . . not liking him, true sons that they were . . .

I never looked to Russia. What was there for me? I had gone to Paris and after Paris . . . of course Gosho lived like a prince in Moscow and yet he wanted to come home to Bulgaria. It is better to be a big fish in a familiar pond than a tiny fish that can become an irritant and   you disappear. I did not ask what had happened to his comrades from the fire. I should have.

The duck was very good. And he has asparagus from god only knows where.   He stuffed us with food. He knew what we had not been eating for years.

He set a good table. I enjoyed the food. I had learned my lesson well in
Paris.

To die with dirty hands and you go on living with dirty hands, just
playing into the hands of those who talk about hearts and you would
think there would be built a monument in the middle of the public baths
just under the painting of Lenin's head

    TO THE CLEAN HANDS OF THE NEW BULGARIA

10th Anniversary of Death of Nikola Petkov

September 20, 1957

**September 23, 1957, marks the 10th anniversary of the
execution of the Bulgarian patriot Nikola Petkov by the Communist regime of Bulgaria. One of the Bulgarian leaders who
signed the armistice in 1944, he helped to end his country's
alliance with Nazi Germany and played a leading role in
establishing a democratic coalition government. He was a
defender of freedom and a champion of the rights of his fellow
Bulgarians. His imprisonment and tragic death allowed the
forces against which he fought to gain control in Bulgaria.**

**The spirit of Nikola Petkov still lives. His devotion to the
cause of democracy is an inspiration to his countrymen and to
all who love freedom. His name is an enduring symbol of hope
to his people and a source of pride and solace to them in this
period of trial.**

Stripped of everything and dressed in clothes given to me, taken from
the last man who was in this room . . . and then those clothes stripped

off of me and given to the next and the next and the next . . . eventually the clothing will be so stiff from ourselves, from the leakings . . . they will use a knife and slice the cloth from the back . . . nothing should be individual about any of the proceedings.

Just another day at work.

Just into the office for the night shift, right Piko?

One more and tomorrow one more and . . . a year or so ago you did them in batches of twenty, up against the wall and a waste of Russian bullets or did they think it was the cheapest way . . . probably got the ammunition from the English . . .

Nothing out of the ordinary. The same light bulb, the same rope . . . the same stool

An editorial statement: The Americans cut bait!

*

From the Acting Representative of the United States in Bulgaria, John E. Horner, to the Secretary of State, Washington, D.C., June 7, 1947, 6 P.M.

While realizing this is matter of high level policy and raises numerous implications I feel gravamen of considerations leading to decision last February (Deptel 44, Feb 4[*13*]) to recognize Bulgarian regime shortly after ratification of peace treaty based on premise there would be effective and reasonably free opposition at that time. If that is so suggest decision be reexamined in context of past several months. . . . To recognize present Bulgarian regime without assiduous effort to obtain specific assurances in advance on such of these questions as Department considers of basic importance would seem great mistake. It would mean writing off Bulgaria and abandoning any hope of implementing Article II of treaty. Believe we should hold up recognition until we are satisfied that minimum of conditions will be met or we should face fact that we will have no influence in this country in future. Middle course of recognizing government with pious statement that we hope they will observe Article II would seem to me to be least desirable alternative.

*

Minutes of the Secretary of State's Staff Meeting, June 9, 1947, 9:30 A.M.

(Secret) A. Political Persecution in the Balkans.

It was further agreed that Minister Maynard Barnes should not as he desires, return to Bulgaria to seek to obtain the release of Petkov, the recently arrested leader of the Agrarian Party.

It was further agreed that the U.S. should not alter its present plan to recognize the Bulgarian government following the coming into force of the peace treaty.

Among those present at the meeting, Dean Acheson, George F. Kennan . . .

I could heap up disgust and live upon a supper of distemper for the rest of . . .

not much longer.

I tried so long to separate the useful from the useless. I really did. Possibly it was a mistake. I should have gone to one extreme or the other. It is to be saddled up and stuck in the middle. A sort of donkey for those to either side of me.

Would a wide floppy hat have saved me?

I am not a religious man. This world is what has to matter. I have no claim on anything else. I never learned of the indifference of seasons, of the rain, of the snow, of the sun.

No lesson in any of this . . . I wish there was . . . of course a lot can be said and will be said. Ain't that always the way it is in this world, this world where I would have been happier . . . but who ever thinks of that when the . . .

Or, was there ever a moment when it could have been different? Who

could have thought it would have turned out this way . . .
Where are the nouns, the particular details   gone I am afraid the
way of newspapers and newspapers formed the rope . . .
Piko is innocent of newspapers. He will hear about what he has done.
He will hear and hear and will have never listened to a single thing. It
will be as if I never existed. Only those . . . far away from this moment
will remember . . . and their memories will become vague, memories
forced to live in mean cities without a mouth connected to an ear able to
hear what is being said

Yes, I came back and knew, probably what was there, if I dared to stop
for one minute . . . did I ever stop for one minute . . . I will not answer
. . . by coming back . . . I knew the rules and they knew the rules and
then the war goes on and on and Boris comes back and is dead through a
spell cast by Adolf . . . surely the peasants know something happened
. . . their explanation is as good as any . . . and I would say peasant
never having the ability to imagine anyone who would ever take insult
at that word: it will happen . . .
And I landed in the camp at Gonda Voda . . . the general says it was by
accident   but then everything we do is by accident. I am not going to
be trapped into defending purposeful activity. I am not THAT stupid.
We are creatures of the wind, of the clouds, of the rivers.
The earth, man, the earth, down to earth . . . if only you had been, there
would be no need to lift you off the earth, off this cement floor . . .
Fly my little bird but remember no bird makes a nest in a cloud.

Honorable Judges! in concluding, I shall consider one more
question. I wish to refute a reproach made to Nikola Petkov. He is
asked: Why do you not confess in the face of so much incriminating
data?
Honorable Judges, one must keep one's eyes closed to some

facts to be able to say such a thing to the defendant. He is entitled by the law not to confess, he has the right to be silent, not to say a thing or everything.

Nikola Petkov has been warned and if he does not seek a way of concealment or escape, I must stress that he is a man who is ready to bear the sanctions of the law and to assume full responsibility for his acts and this is noble.

Honorable Judges, he is accused of serving reaction, some domestic reaction. Do not forget that there is nothing stronger than blood, and between him and reaction is the grave and blood of his brother.

Honorable Judges, in passing your sentence, consider these arguments of mine. Whatever it be, it is the sentence of a Bulgarian court, before which my client is a Bulgarian citizen, and not a traitor. He appeared before the court to receive it. He will bear it, because from him who has been given much, much is expected. He will bear it with dignity, because he respects and honors the Bulgarian court. With this confidence he will await for your verdict tomorrow.

I plead for acquittal.

And the world does not cease to exist when I . . .

and much later someone will write
               I left the train at five o'clock in the afternoon. That is what I have always said, I left the train at five o'clock . . . even began a poem called "Bulgaria" in that manner . . . walked from the station and years later ran into this name Nikola Petkov and in McDaid's after being told this guy had a friend who went to Bulgaria and fell off a mountain—you should read your man Shaw's play Arms and the Man *. . . there you have another Petkov . . . I don't know if they spell it the same way . . .*

and reasons slip away . . . no use holding on . . . there has never been

any use in holding on   things must take their course ... no use in
hurrying or in delay.
Basil plucked out Bulgarian eyes. It is my mistake to think something
had not happened to ears at the same time. A people strangely affected
by the loss of both eyes and ears. Our tongues still work. Mine almost
stopped.
Almost. Almost. Almost.

As regards the accused Nikola Petkov, however, it seems to me that nobody could put on the scales of the balance of justice a single attenuating circumstance.

Having taken a wrong path since the very day of the historical act of September 9, he did not stop on the threshold of honor, but dishonored our country. Identifying like an absolutist his proper interests with those of our country, he reneged his own self. A French king once declared:"The State—it is me!" This was the end of a historical epoch.

Nikola Petkov is the very spirit of negation, bearing the torch of civil war.

History is not made by egoists who do not see their country there where they are not.

The contempt of generations is not sufficient to efface his activity as disclosed before us.

The bench of the accused on which he sits, will be a bench of eternal opprobium.

No sanction is to punish such an activity.

At a moment when our fatherland calls out and the laws stipulate, you will find sufficient reasons to impose the supreme penalty.

The end of one person is preferable to that of the collectivity.

He who organized a blow against the State must get the supreme penalty which he deserves.

Freedom demands his punishment!

Therefore, I beg you, Honorable Judges, to pronounce a sentence in this sense.

Symbolic incitement . . . choked. The classical world thrown at my
head. To duck was to fall into a pit of shit . . . down there to wrestle with
squabbling worms . . . at least they will not chop off my hands and peel
away face from skull as they will Gosho . . . to lie there in his air-
conditioned display case . . . usually
                                    REMONT
an awful sort of church. Allow some café professor to work out the
parallels, the jokes, the icons of chopped-off hands and a mask of flesh:
what did they stretch the skin over, attach the hands to . . . what sort of
makeup. Enough times in the theater and have seen enough corpses on
the stage . . .
Forced . . . the ceiling is panelled. I didn't notice that before . . . a
blonde sort of wood.

Not to go on living.
Just another corpse clogging up the drainage system of the planet to
echo an American thief on his own deathbed—how I envy him his bed
or that man who just simply dies in a dark corner of an abandoned
building or behind a wall under a tree.
However just alive for some period of time and now no longer
alive.
Not able to expand Piko's part in this dramatic scene of a stage stripped
back to the brick wall, workmen can be seen moving about, actors
waiting to move into the bright lights, the lightman at his console, the
friends of first night waiting to see if . . . and I would have to be standing
on an abstract chair, the rope, the shadow of the bracelet on the back
wall . . . the sound of water dripping or some sort of modern music;
Piko walking midst his empty buckets . . .
The bright lights and so few words   the audience gets nervous . . .
nervous, I hope, instead of bored.

A show trial to be sure but none of the histrionics one could expect. There was to be no grand speech like Robert Emmet from the dock, just before: torn apart and his heart chewed up by the dogs of the street. This is a civilized country and in a civilized time. A man is not hanged, drawn, quartered, his spirit released to God.

No memorable flight of language for future generations to soar into . . . They had chosen well. Words never did come easily to me. I could not think on my feet, as some are known to do. I had to wait and then . . .

I had my taste of the country and you can always keep me forever in the city. To lie in a country place . . . never. I need the sound of streetcars, the sounds of all those songs of American movies from the 1930s . . . I need to smell foreign places when I walk down the street.

Remember in Svishtov to even walk those mean little streets . . . was a certain pleasure and I had my two faithful dogs at my heels. The only pleasure being able to walk the roundabout way to the station to say I was here and am still here and will be back in four hours to say again I am here and have been here and will be here in another four hours when I tell them I am going home to sleep and they will have to come to see me in my sleep when I make room in my dreams to report I am here and I will be here in four hours and I have been here for the last four hours no matter what they have heard to the contrary.

To talk of regret would be to forgive myself with poetry. I cannot reach for language. I cannot reach for song. I must . . . I have to do nothing. That is my end. I have come to the moment when I can do nothing. There was never a moment when I . . .

I can hear the leaves bouncing off my head, the sound of rain, of a breeze, of a woman's hair against the sunlight . . . throw in some sort of animal, crippled by an automobile . . .

I was a person who went along . . . where is the crime in that . . . where is the virtue to be struck down

I should have gone to Sweden. I should have gone to Norway. There would have been the adventure of Iceland and even Denmark was a place people made expeditions to, even as armies of citizens from those countries cluttered the streets of Paris looking for the light . . . and Finns were there but I could not form an idea about who they were. To sit in a train compartment, by myself, going north in Sweden to be alone, finally in a real forest . . . however I could not be THAT alone. I was alone in Paris sitting in the Café Flore . . . alone with those other Bulgarians who said they were there to paint, to write, who said and who said and who said   that is all they did and I sat and said nothing . . . alone but not as alone as I would be in a compartment alone in a train going north in Sweden . . .

Harritena wanted to be a nun. I do not know the whole story, even now and never will . . . does it matter. Lying in bed she talked about singing in the choir, of the music that made her love those moments; but these smells. Why didn't people bathe, to think they were in the choir and still they didn't bathe . . . to go away, that is all she wanted and I had done the same and come back and should have gone further away . . . but who knows . . . no one does . . . I will answer for myself . . . green eyes, she had, to slide into poetry through twisting of the language . . . allow a lie into the room, as if the room were not already filled with lies, lies, lies and my own death, a lie.
I have said it. My own death. I should begin to speak of myself in the past tense . . . as if I had not always thought of myself in the past tense . . . because people always saw me in the past tense . . . back there—in the blood of my brother, in my father's blood.

South Slavdom, Slavdom, brotherly Russia and freedom loving democratic peoples . . . green cheese from the moon, shit turning into gold in the toilets of The Bambouk, urine into cognac . . . wrinkles into the smiles of a young woman just about to remove her undergarments . . . this rope into the fingers of Harritena as she said goodbye to me walking in front of the Nevski Cathedral; she had to run . . . her mother was waiting for her . . . her father was dead, her brothers dead, her sister dead . . . she lived in the altar of the dead . . . as did I . . .
Piko would light a cigarette but he has none. He has been getting nervous . . . this should be getting to an end and fast, and fast. It will be his head next. He could . . . for a cigarette . . . that is what he needs . . . well to begin with . . .

Wrapping a wool scarf about my neck as I stepped from the door into Vitosha Boulevard after leaving Harritena . . . after seeing a pool of menstrual blood or . . . no, it was not a pool, just the water was cloudy with her blood   a walking away   it was   walking away. That is all I could do. What could I offer . . . best to remember and then . . . regret lasts longer than any pleasure   or the memory of any pleasure.
The novels I have read do not lend themselves to memory or quotation though I am sure there are some . . . to think he knew *Gone With the Wind* . . . and poor Nevena with her hundred translated novels . . . and not one surviving into print today . . . into any—

Venice calls. Ah, Turgenev, no one will fault me for calling in your name. *The Diary of a Useless Man* . . . there was a moment in Moscow when I asked Gosho if he had ever read Rozanov. Gosho was startled. I did not pursue the question. *Scattered Leaves* and no leaves in this room, not even the hint of nature   save for the farts of Piko

I have lived in the centrality of my nervous system and Piko was given orders that it was not to be severed at my end . . . I was to have the life gasped out of me . . . to be fully conscious until the last moment. The sentences will not fall apart. They will not have THAT satisfaction. I am alive until . . .

It was always how to reach out . . . echoing something said in church . . . platitudes of beggars and imagining ourselves there by the side of the road   and all the vanity of imagining ourselves with a bowl "and eyes that . . ."

But I did not lust for pleasure, for comfort. It was not in my nature. Oh, they did not nail me to the wall and have beautiful young women come and lick the sweat from my back . . .

                                        Gosho is sound asleep. One more bit of the road is torn up

                                how's that for obscurity . . . good or fine enough for Yavarov

what is noble is always in a state of humiliation

Man is *temporary*. Who can endure this idea . . .

The meaning does not lie in the eternal; it lies in the moments. Moments are eternal, while eternity is only "their environment." An apartment for a lodger. The moment is the lodger, the moment is "I," the sun.

        Making love or riding a motorcycle, it's all the same. Each
    moment has its stereotype, and fragments of time carry off
    fragments of men into a past that can never be changed.
        What's the use of threading pearls to make a garland of
    memories? If only the weight of the pearls would snap the thread!
    But no: moment by moment, time bores on; everything is lost,

nothing created . . .

What do I want? Not a succession of moments, but one huge instant. A totality that is lived, and without the experience of "time passing." The feeling of "time passing" is simply the feeling of growing old. And yet, since one must survive in order to live, virtual moments, possibilities, are necessarily rooted in that time. When we try to federate moments, to bring out the pleasure in them, to release their promise of life, we are already learning how to construct "situations."

No one is ever around when . . . even if the news is bad . . . so they can tell you about the time . . . Piko, stop laughing! Oh, please stop laughing. Please . . .

no, go right ahead. It is your freedom, your way to place me. As I should have placed myself. I did not trust my comfort. I did not trust my books, my own life.

Was it in the Hotel de Dream that I met Mr. Crane? He said he was no relation to the American writer. It was all a matter of coincidence that if you read it in a book . . . you would not believe it. Mr. Crane told me of his home in Wisconsin . . . we don't have many Bulgarians in our state. They live in Illinois and in Indiana. Must have had something to do with the cold or . . . I really don't know. You are the first Bulgarian I have met and I am sorry to say the only thing I know about your country is that Sofia is the capital and that your armies did terrible things to the Greeks.

If you believe your writer Hemingway, I replied. In Bulgaria only the communists believed Hemingway and even they are having their doubts . . . but I don't like his prose . . . though he does have interesting emotions; can I say that in English?

You can say anything you damn well please in American, Mr. Crane
said . . . and I said it must be an interesting country where you can say
anything you damn well please. How do people understand each other?
As well as in any other country or people, only we don't listen carefully
to each other.

                        nothing of Mr. Crane remains except the pounding of
his fingertips against the top of the table. His fingers were very long and
the tip of each finger was like a dulled ceremonial bayonet.
You did not, Piko, have to hit the soles of my feet with that length of
wood. There is still feeling enough . . .

One could expect the wall to give way and find Gosho crashing into the
room, just to make sure . . . at least he won't have to worry about him
any more . . . no virtue to protect. None to steal. Thank God or
whoever the woman was . . . can I remember. AM I expected to
remember . . .
Only possible to give way to farce.
The rope would break.
Piko would die of a heart attack or get the hots and climb on for a quick
fuck.
No erections, yet. No mocking jest. Can I say: it is coming . . . and
leave the ambiguity there as to what it refers to . . .

Everything comes to the end of one sort or another. And there is just
nothing . . .
No tolling of a bell, somewhere in the haze of the middle of night . . . or
is that morning . . . early morning when the sky goes ink blue . . . dark
ink blue . . . or some such color . . . a black eye . . .
fiddle music from somewhere.

Just so pathetic. No family at the foot of the bed, no grumbling servants in the hallway . . . what is a hallway for except to have servants prowl it waiting . . . waiting is what they are good at; what we are all good for just waiting   even these frail minutes   a lie in the adjective *frail* minutes as if time had muscles to be developed . . . only muscle is the one between my ears allowing me to come back to this country, to these clean streets . . . these awful clean streets . . . and all of them at the foot of my bed wondering how much longer they are going to have to stand there, when will I get it over with, how much money are they going to receive for their services at my death agony   and I will leave them NOTHING   that is what they deserve   nothing   no, this is all not true   I am trapped in the lie of death   of this death reception . . . something awful   like a radio broadcast not clearly heard   no longer able to say   it will go on

*

PREMIER GEORGI DIMITROV REFUTES FOREIGN
ATTACKS REGARDING NIKOLA PETKOV'S
EXECUTION

*

I must emphasize that the Bulgarian people in their large majority approved the verdict against Nikola Petkov and its execution. In this sense, the papers published the declarations of the National Committee of the Fatherland Front, the Central Committees, of the General Workers' Professional Union, the General Agrarian Professional Union, the General Craft's Professional Union, the Democratic Youth, the Central Managements of many workers' professional unions, the Union of Bulgarian Lawyers, 15 academicians, 67 professors, and many other intellectual workers, the Union of Musicians, the Jewish Central Consistory in Bulgaria, the Administrative Council of the Chamber of National Culture, the artists of the National Theatre, etc. The newspapers were deluged with telegrams from different women's, youth's, cooperative, professional and party organizations, resolutions of mass meetings, condemning the activity of

Nikola Petkov and approving the verdict.

For the Bulgarian Government and personally for me, it is this fact that has a decisive meaning, rather than the slanderous campaign abroad, obviously reflecting the aggressive intentions of the imperialist circles against the nations which struggle for their freedom, independence and final consolidation of their peoples democracy and their State sovereignty.

*

As regards Nikola Petkov's clemency, it was politically impossible, after the rude attempt of the British and American representatives in Sofia at intervening in the activity of the sovereign Bulgarian Court. It can be said outright that these interventions have a great share of responsibility for Nikola Petkov's fate. The execution of the verdict should serve as a lesson to all who, out of egoistic interests or under foreign suggestion, wish to bury the freedom, attained at the cost of so many dear victims. Only soft people, who have not experienced the horrors of a monarcho-fascist dictatorship and foreign yoke, or of malignant enemies could see in the action of the Bulgarian Court of Justice an expression of vengeance or cruelty toward their political opponents. Nikola Petkov's execution is a legal self-defense of the young People's Republic Bulgaria against the attempts of the reactionary forces, supported from abroad, to turn back the clock of history.

*

The second category of demarches on behalf of Nikola Petkov come from reactionary individuals and groups hostile to new democratic Bulgaria and to everything progressive the world over. It is not the personal fate of Nikola Petkov that concerns these people. They merely take advantage of his process to launch a new slanderous campaign against our People's Republic, the USSR and the Eastern European People's Democracies as well as against the communists in their own countries. The world reactionaries hastened to take Nikola Petkov under their protective wing.

*

From the beginning to the end, Nikola Petkov's whole political capital, which helped him assume one of the leading positions in the Agrarian Union, was the heroic death of his brother, killed by the fascists. But the difference between him and his brother is boundless. Under Nikola Petkov's leadership the opposition Agrarian Union became a center of the most reactionary and fascist elements. It was those elements and the suggestions of certain foreigners who incited him toward conspirative and terrorist activity. For the information of the public regarding the data brought up at the process, the Government has undertaken to publish in English and French all stenographic protocols of the process. These people must realize that is was not out of revenge, or cruelty, but on account of an imperative state necessity that the People's Republic Bulgaria could not in the present moment manifest any indulgence toward people convicted by the sovereign Bulgarian Court of Justice in preparing a coup d'Etat.

*

Dimiter Stoyanov, former organizational Secretary of the Union, in a statement admits that Nikola Petkov aimed at disorganizing the economic life of the country, by creating unrest, in order to provoke foreign intervention. To this effect, certain foreigners had promised Nikola Petkov their support. Stoyanov condemns this activity of Petkov as injurious, anti-national, anti-Soviet and treacherous.

*

The former deputy, Todora Koeva, declared that Nikola Petkov's activity, dictated by foreign representatives in our country, is anti-national, anti-Slav and treacherous.

*

Peter Surbinsky, Secretary of Nikola Petkov's Agrarian Youth Union, declares in a statement, published in the papers, that he condemns Nikola Petkov's policy—a policy of delivering information to foreigners, of plots and conspiracies. Such a policy, he declares, is not peasant policy, but hostile and treacherous.

Nothing comes back . . . literature is of not much use. Well, then, what is of use? What do you mean by *use?*
The flesh swells over the handcuffs, the flesh swells over the rope.
The warm shit, the urine . . . but no tears. Don't worry. No tears . . . no

asking for . . .

They had no need to beat me. Yet they did. I fell, as someone wrote down. Down I fell. I had difficulty walking because I had become weighed down with my guilt. The guilt kept tripping me up . . . or so they said.

I'll tell you any story you want to hear or not hear depending on your view of the storyteller.

I would like to blow my nose.

I would like to blow my nose.

To be a haiduk in the mountains and I always thought where do they shit in the middle of the epic being recited.

A child's question not much suited, does not reflect well on an adult . . . can't you elevate your mind for this, your last moments . . . where does a haiduk shit?

Only a dilettante, a person of what shall we call it . . . a question a man of the streets might ask   or a fatalistic dilettante—

Heroism terrifies me. And I will be seen as such . . . the further away a person is from a hero the taller the tower upon which to place him, the longer the shit has to fall before it hits the upturned face.

They will bury me six foot under and in a grave . . . who after the second generation will even know where it is . . .

a winter day walking in a village, I forget which village . . . snow heaped up and the sun blazing and someone had been there just before me by the look of the snow . . . only one other set of footprints and had nailed a death notice to the weathered fence in front of the church . . . no picture . . . just a name I have forgotten and a date which I have also forgotten . . . a cross, of course . . . so eager to get the notice of the death out . . . get it out of the room in which the person . . .

President:—Mr. Petkov, do you wish to speak?

Defendant Nikola Petkov:—I wish to have the last word.

President:—At the last pleading we will give you only 5–6 minutes.

Defendant Nikola Petkov:—I will not take more than 5–6 minutes in order not to tire the public with long speeches. I have everything written here.

Honorable Judges! After hearing the testimony of the witnesses, the speeches of the Prosecution and the Defense, I declare with a clear conscience and fully conscious of my responsibility, before the Bulgarian Justice, before the public as well as before my political organization, to which I belong and for which I am always ready to give my life, that I have never engaged or thought of engaging in illegal activity against the People's Government after September 9, 1944, in the creation of which participated both the Agrarian Union and I personally.

I forsook the Fatherland Front—which is not correct—and came out in opposition not on my volition, but by decision of the Presidiums of the Bulgarian Agrarian National Union. From the time of my coming out in opposition until my detention I have worked for the collaboration of the Agrarian Union and the Workers Party (C) which I consider a historical necessity.

I have never been engaged in serving any reaction, be it internal or foreign.

Honorable Judges! I am sure that you will set aside politics, because it has no place in this hall of justice. I am sure that you will bear in mind only the positively established facts. Being certain that you will be guided exclusively by the truth and by your judicial conscience, I hope you will issue against me a verdict of acquittance.

Fifty-five years of this life.

Untie the fucker and wash off the rope. I have to have a little professional flair in this job. Don't like using a dirty rope on any man. Was on orders to use the same rope as on the guys from yesterday. Who does he think he is, they said . . . a clean rope . . . would he have given us a clean rope . . . he can't even nod his head in an attempt at rebuttal . . . he probably didn't even have it in him to see his enemies done into the ground, that is what you have to do—have them done into the ground . . .

wash down the stool, wash down the floor, wash my hands and take a drink.   Not out of any consideration, but I have to be in this room more times than any of them . . . for a longer period of time, no sense having to wade across, might slip and break my neck . . . hangman breaks own neck . . . pass the raki . . . the hangman breaks his own neck . . . pass the raki

his eyes close; they will snap open, finally

I might have . . .

That's enough. I've had enough. I can't take it anymore. Just on and on. That's what happens . . . loves his own voice, his own thoughts and ends up with an audience of one: the hangman.

A fish no longer struggling. Caught in a broken net   and on top of everything. Should keep the nets repaired.

Tell it to the boss. Complaint forms are just outside the door. If you can get that far.

I might . . .

Though I said, I have had enough. Just air being moved about. No more time for final speeches and anyway they only happen in the movies. No one is around to take down the final words. Just gurgle on and . . .

The fish does not respond to the little boy poking it with a stick.

"Nothing and everything."

Is that it?

sense of being cheated, no setting sun, no final . . .

SENTENCE

On the contrary, Nikola Petkov is not just anybody. He is a former Minister without Portfolio in the first F. F. Government, former member of the National F. F. Committee, a public figure, journalist, jurist and leader of part of the opposition in this country. Nikola Petkov is one of the creators of the

Law on the Defense of the People's Power. By instigating Colonels Ivanov and Gergov to form a conspirative organization in the Bulgarian people's army, he undermined the greatest factor of our State security and that at a most crucial moment for our State, when the unity of the army was more necessary than ever. Prisoner of his lust for power, he was ready to throw our country into the flames of civil war. In appraising all these circumstances with a view to establishing the degree of defendant Nikola Petkov's guilt, the court finds that they aggravate his guilt. That is why, in determining the punishment for the defendant, the court, availing itself of the sovereign power given to it by the law, chooses the second and graver alternative and absolutely determined sanction—death through hanging and to pay 500,000 leva fine to the State treasury to be replaced, in case of insolvency, by 6 months imprisonment, depriving him of the rights under art. 30 of the Penal Law for life.

REJECTION OF APPEAL AGAINST SENTENCE

Under the rule of absorbtion (of the less severe crimes by the most severe crime committed by the accused) and in virtue of Art. 64 of the Penal Law for the crimes committed by Nikola D. Petkov under Art. 1 paragraph I of the Decree Law on the Defense of the People's Power in connection with Art. 51, paragraph 2 of the Penal Law, under Art. 3 of the Law on the Defense of the People's Power in connection with art. 51, paragraph II of the Penal Law, under Art. 6 and 7 paragraph I and III of the Decree Law on the Defense of the People's Power, the Court determines for him a single punishment—death through hanging and to pay a fine of 500,000 leva to the State Treasury, replaceable in case of insolvency by six months imprisonment, divesting him of the rights under Art. 30 of the Penal Law for always.

maybe, he was showing character

he was just stupid

New York
25 October 1983

Ipek Palas, Istanbul
12 October 1985